PRAISE FOR T]

Henry Gould's remarkable *Green Radius* is not quite like anything else. This huge, slowly-rolling poem of the Mississippi draws us in the course of its 132 individual pieces (plus coda and preface) from January to December 2023. Broadly modernist in its blend of myth, history, scripture, quotation and personal material, its sinuous length is made beguilingly readable by the recurring form of its wave-like stanzas. This story of the river — of the trees that become vessels upon the river, of the men and women on those vessels — is also a story of the river of time and of song, looking back to poetry as ancient as Homer, Pindar, Virgil and Catullus 64, but also across time and languages to more recent predecessors, such as Villon, Baudelaire, Coleridge, Celan, Yeats, Crane and Walcott. Gould's river has, moreover, several presiding geniuses, almost local divinities, including Martin Luther King, Shakespeare's Hamlet and Ophelia, the scriptural Moses, Jonah and Jesus, Abraham Lincoln, John Berryman, the architect Benjamin Latrobe, Nicholas of Cusa and the poet's own ancestors. Each individual poem is dated and placed in chronological order, so the greater poem follows the course of the year, but the poetic mood is markedly static — or perhaps stately is the better word. In its sweep and seriousness and the jewelled care of its style, its attention to each moment, The Green Radius reminded me rather of the Sanskrit *mahakavya*, or 'great poems', in which each stanza or set of stanzas can be read and enjoyed as individual poems, as well as part of the larger mythological narrative. It is a unique and compelling encounter: this river is, as the poem says 'addictive (much like song)'.

– Victoria Moul, Professor of Early Modern
Latin & English, University College London

In *The Green Radius*, Henry Gould seeks solace and revelation on the banks of the Mississippi. He sounds its depths and calls down the ancestors for guidance and wisdom, as he broods over this troubled nation with a river in its heart – a river that divides but also gathers, that brings ruin but also brings forth life.

Gould invites us to sail with him: "Help me discern, reader, my own dark meaning!" Like all good river journeys, *The Green Radius* is meandering, sinuous, meditative. It is a deeply moving rumination on heartbreak and hope – part song and part spell.

– Robert van Vliet, author of Vessels

Gould's poetry is like lucid dreaming. Dream-logic but the poet is an agent. An agent who trusts the dream. As the pilot has to trust the river. You can know some things to steer toward, some to avoid, but you can't know everything. It's the river that moves the boat, according to its own preoccupations: the spirituality of a nation, the memories of one person, the history of a land.

– J-T Kelly, author of Like Now

Of all the ways this long poem is like the river it celebrates – its shape of meander, its immediacy and liquified history, its breadth and detail – what I like best is the way it hypnotizes, with sparkle on bright surface, and with mystery. The poem does not dwell on the physical dangers of the big river – but in its drift and swell, the treacherous undercurrents of the nation's ominous moral situation are mirrored. *The Green Radius* offers a lively exploration of the muddy depths that the living river cannot – because, though bound, the true Mississippi is never tamed. If it can be contained in a work of art, though, this book is that container. If you love rivers, read *The Green Radius*.

– Kyla Houbolt, author of But Then I Thought

The sonar's green line sweeps its circle and picks up local movements and waves that have been rippling in consciousness for hundreds of years — it keeps its own rhythm and pings its private landmarks hypnotically, obsessively, reassuringly, in a code made to be broken. Henry Gould is the latest master poet of American place, from the Brain Sciences Center, to the home of Mardi Gras, to Nineveh.

– Jordan Davis

THE GREEN RADIUS

*

Henry Gould

Contubernales Books

2024

ISBN : 978-1-961822-15-3

ACKNOWLEDGEMENTS

The author gratefully acknowledges publication of portions of this work in the journals *Subtropics, Trampoline, Dusie, Touch the Donkey, Orphic Review,* and *Tourniquet Review.*

Special thanks to Gabriel Gudding and A.M. Juster : poets, translators, friends.

Cover illustration [front and back], courtesy of Saint Louis Art Museum :John J. Egan, American (born Ireland), 1810–1882; *Twelve Gated Labyrinth, Missouri; Indians at Their Piscatory Exploits, scene seven from Panorama of the Monumental Grandeur of the Mississippi Valley,* c.1850; distemper on cotton muslin; 90 inches x 348 feet; Saint Louis Art Museum, Eliza McMillan Trust 34:1953

Frontispiece : courtesy of Hennepin County Library. "Sea Scout training ship *Pegasus* on the Mississippi River" [*Minneapolis Star Journal*, August 27, 1940].

TABLE OF CONTENTS

PREFACE

Poetry is a mystery. A mystery equally to poets as to everyone else. Keats' notion of "negative capability" is a brief and elegant gesture toward that vast, vague, undiscovered realm.

We might say that poetry is a work of song, insight and imagination. Triggered in the poet as much by trance and rapture, as by reason and intellect. Poets step into a verbal river... and find themselves simultaneously swept along and struggling upstream.

Poetry, in America, is a kind of double or triple mystery; a cryptic box, with more than one false bottom. To sense this, we need only glance at the riddling originality of Poe, Melville, Dickinson and Whitman. As Roy Harvey Pearce noted long ago (Continuity of American Poetry, 1961), U.S. culture is a clash of contraries : between prophetic enthusiasm on the one hand, and practical "business sense" on the other. So its poetry blossomed in a contrarian antithesis : opposing both heavy-handed religion, and crass utilitarian Mammon, at the same time.

Paul Valéry famously described poetry as an "abuse of language". Ordinary language, practical language, good language, useful language – just like ordinary, practical, good, useful people – disappears into the work it accomplishes; whereas poetry does the opposite. It coils like a whirlpool, like a serpent, like a vortex, back on itself – for the sake of something supremely impractical. Let's call it the eternal Sabbath of the human imagination. Let's call it the irenic dream of the riverboat, the canoe, the drifter, the yearning hobo in our midst – the human soul. But... an abuse of language? Osip Mandelstam, in a poem addressed to Anna Akhmatova, wrote : "Preserve my speech, for its taste of sadness and smoke." Poetry strengthens and gives life to language – merely by slowing it down, focusing its intensity, and... by recitation... revealing its depths, its glories, its power.

Ten years ago, we moved from Providence, RI – where I had spent most of my life – back to my hometown, Minneapolis. And not just to my hometown, but to the very blocks where I had first babbled baby sounds, the streets where my parents, grandparents, and great-grandparents had lived, for 150 years. "Southeast", near the University and Tower Hill; across the street from the Mississippi (East River Road).

Rivers are subtle, serpentine. They mimic the variable pulse of time itself, in order to do something else. And poetry mimics the mimic. Verse veers, burbles... poetry flows... so as to move (in imagination, intellect) upstream, against the current.

Since moving back in 2015, I have spent many hours ambling along that riverbank, below the ravine, across the street. I finished another anaconda-length sequence I had begun in Rhode Island (Ravenna Diagram, vols. I-III), and a third book-length poem, looking back through a Rhode Island lens (Restoration Day). But this most recent work struck a new note. Over these recent years, I've observed with foreboding the threat from within – forces on the move against the very idea of America. The force of greed, the force of callousness, the force of violence... the force of force itself. Against the equilibrium of that spiritual America Walt Whitman celebrated : "Perennial with the Earth, with Freedom, Law, and Love". Of America as "itself the greatest Poem". Such an America is a democratic ideal, an idea. But this country, in tandem with its idea, is also a land. A physical, geographical, planetary place. As that crotchety Yankee nationalist Robert Frost put it, in his ambiguous way : "The land was ours before we were the land's." It is here, for me, in this context, that the Mississippi River comes in.

I began this poem in late January, 2023, while brooding about the shallow hatreds, energized by corrupt political actors, that were (and are) tearing us apart as a people. And I thought of this ancient, muddy river, running down the center of the land, as a wounded heart, bleeding from red/blue veins. And I searched for dimensions which were part of the flow, but resisted the flow : other times, other places, that seemed to point in the same direction. Places like old French America, with its faintly Gallic medieval overtone (the Seine, the Loire)... adrift down to Louisiana. Hidden there from the beginning, I realized – when the opening passage points to an early Eric Rohmer film, Le Rayon Vert (The Green Ray). Curiously, just after finishing the poem (at the end of 2023) I happened to watch another classic Rohmer film, My Night at Maud's. So, cher lecteur, I hope you will enjoy some things in my long voyage... enjoy them almost as much as you might enjoy those old French films.

Minneapolis
February 19, 2024
(President's Day)

POSTSCRIPT

Poetry is make-believe. A fiction, woven by imagination and desire (the heart's desire, the mind's imagination). This was forcefully brought home to me over Easter weekend, by a message from an old Rhode Island friend, a poet and professor, who sent me his response after reading *The Green Radius.* He questioned why, in a work which opens with an apostrophe to three great Native American leaders, and which includes repeated invocations of Black Elk, Cahokia, the legend of Turtle-Woman, and other images of Native America, that nevertheless there is no concrete focus on the actual history of U.S./Native tribal relations – a history which glares with a massive power imbalance, scarred with chauvinism, animosity, and cultural suppression. In a poem which evokes the uncommon grandeur of a shared land, the often-fraudulent terms of that inheritance are never presented. How much suffering and injustice lie hidden beneath the first half of that famous Robert Frost line quoted above! "The land was ours..."

And I suddenly realized how my poem's terms were limited by my own cultural hedges : those of a person of European ancestry, whose family came to settle in America (in Topsfield, Massachusetts) in 1635. And that the chance my country has, even to begin to step forward – toward justice, friendship and reconciliation – will only be granted when we can say, with both word and deed : "The land was *not* ours."

I am grateful to my friend and fellow poet for his kindly word to the wise.

April 1, 2024
(April Fools' Day)

FROM THE HEADWATERS

by Gabriel Gudding

On May 11 2024, as this book was going to print, the state of Minnesota, where *The Green Radius* was written, officially changed the image and motto of its state seal after 175 years of controversy and outrage, the outrage stemming from an issue critical to *The Green Radius.*

Minnesota chose on May 11, 2024 to remove from its state seal an image allegorizing the genocide of Native people in the Minnesota territory. May 11 is now a proud day for Minnesota because though the violence against Natives was brutal everywhere in the Americas, it took on a particular and unique blend of terror and systematic evil in Minnesota.

I don't know if Henry Gould ever thought much about the flag and state seal of Minnesota, but his book seems to directly address the Native rider depicted in it. This is the very same rider Mary Henderson Eastman addresses in a poem of 1850, one year after the image was adopted, in a poem she called "The State Seal of Minnesota," published in what is now credited by the Library of Congress as the first newspaper of the territory, *The Minnesota Pioneer.* Eastman was wife of the Army artist, Seth Eastman, who twice served at Fort Snelling, once as its commander, and who painted in watercolor the original image of the seal. So if anyone was to have a handle on what was intended by the image, she was.

The image on the flag and seal for 175 years, up until only a few days ago, depicts a white settler ploughing in the foreground, an ax and a musket leaning against a stump, while in the background a Native on horseback is perpetually leaving the scene, constantly galloping into the sunset. The fact of this image, painted at Fort Snelling, only five miles from where Gould writes this book, is of utmost pertinence to *The Green Radius.*

As if to remove any ambiguity about the image as to the violence intended against Natives, Eastman penned an 8-stanza 64-line ekphrastic poem called "The Seal of Minnesota," that speaks directly to the Native in the image, ordering him nine times to "give way" and leave Minnesota.[1] It starts:

> Give way, give way young warrior,
> Thou and thy steed give way —
> Rest not, though lingers on the hills,
> The red sun's parting ray.
> The rocky bluff and prairie land
> The white man claims them now,
> The symbols of his course are here,
> The rifle, axe and plough.
> ....

and continues, speaking then both about him and again to him:

> We claim his noble heritage,
> And Minnesota's land
> Must pass with all its untold wealth
> To the white man's grasping hand.
> ....
> Thou and thy noble race from earth
> Must soon be passed away,
> As echoes die upon the hills,
> Or darkness follows day.

This poem is one of many pieces in the cupboards of American literature that speak either to or about (sometimes both, as in Eastman's poem) Native Americans as if they were and are destined to be denizens of the past. Henry Wadsworth Longfellow's "The Song of Hiawatha" of 1855 follows suit by adumbrating, with a certain degree of what can be construed as admiration and respect, their inevitable decline. Philip Freneau's "The Indian Burying

---

[1] *Minnesota Pioneer*, February 20, 1850

Ground" of 1787 manages to sustain a melancholic tone even as it already laments, all too soon laments, the passing away of "the fancies of a ruder race" as he looks at petroglyphs, while William Cullen Bryant's poem of 1832, "The Prairies," speaks of Native people as part of a vanished past:

> "Are they here—
> The dead of other days?—and did the dust
> Of these fair solitudes once stir with life
> And burn with passion? Let the mighty mounds
> That overlook the rivers, or that rise
> In the dim forest crowded with old oaks,
> Answer. A race, that long has passed away,
> Built them ...."

To Bryant, they might be here, but if they are, they are dead. Joseph K. Dixon's supposed nonfiction account of 1913 *The Vanishing Race: The Last Great Indian Council* purports to recount "from their speeches and folklore tales, their solemn farewell." For three decades the pioneering ethnographic photographer Edward Sheriff Curtis (1868-1952), whose photographs now hang in the Smithsonian, documented Native American tribes, consistently characterizing Natives as doomed, in his 20-volume lifework *The North American Indian.*

The great Norwegian-American novelist O. E. Rølvaag, who taught for years at St. Olaf's in Northfield, Minnesota, writes similarly in the past tense (or in what could be construed as the genocidal conjugation: *the fading tense*) about the Dakota people in his 1925 novel *Giants in the Earth*, which he wrote only forty miles from Gould's home on the banks of the Mississippi, where he writes *The Green Radius.*

Whether Gould's book begins as an address to that same Native in Seth Eastman's image or in Mary Henderson Eastman's poem, or not, it may as well be said to, because Gould is from an old Minnesota family, and he wrote his book literally a block and a half from the east bank of the Mississippi River, five river miles, exactly, north of Fort Snelling. Fort Snelling, situated prominently on the east bank, served as a deadly base of operations against the Ho-Chunk and Dakota people for decades, where at one point the US Army was offering in 1863 a $200 bounty for every Native scalp brought to the fort by non-military personnel. Gould's house on the riverbank is only 80 miles from the Minnesota River at Mankato where occurred on December 26 1862 the single largest mass government execution in American history, the collective hanging of 38 Dakota men for participating in warfare against the United States government, which had in 1858 dissolved their reservation along both banks of the Minnesota River, taking first the north side then the south side, this was after the federal government had "given" the land (after stealing it) in 1851.

So it is fair to say that Gould's book, *The Green Radius*, sits at the ideological and geographic center of a welter of frankly unfathomable violence and confusion and sorrow and heartache and terror and rape and scalping and sheer rage and harrowing brutality and indifference. And it is is almost as if Gould is purposefully taking up the thought experiment left by the Minnesota state seal and over 250 years of European-descent people writing about and narrativizing Natives.

Gould says in his preface that he wrote *The Green Radius* to counter, to write a balm, a spell, a poem to answer those "forces on the move against the very idea of America. The force of greed, the force of callousness, the force of violence ... the force of force itself. Against the equilibrium of that spiritual America Walt Whitman celebrated" ... the America of the "democratic ideal, an idea." And Gould is fair to point out that contemporary America's current violence, callousness and greed, begins there: in our genocidal past.

Gould's book seems to ask, How does a white writer, a European-descent (a creole) writer, write a poetry cognizant of the history of fascism without first confronting this core genocidal trope? If a

European-descent American writer is interested in, as he says in his preface quoting Whitman, "Freedom, Law, and Love" where do they, in America and specifically in Minnesota, begin?

If we are to write our collective way out of (or rewrite our collective existence from within) the violence and indifference characterizing our era, Gould seems to suggest, which has crescendoed only naturally in Trumpism, we must look squarely into our fascist and genocidal past and most directly at the ways white writers have contributed to this genocide by ideologically preparing the reading public by making the demise of Native people seem natural and inevitable. Gould seems to begin his entire book by taking up this thought experiment where Eastman left off, speaking it seems directly to the same Native as Eastman, in the first first line of his book:

> They have gathered your feathers under glass.
> Your arrowheads have become a collection.
> What was freedom has evolved into. . . perfection.
> Archives trace a cold trail (of wild grass).
>
> I roam from exhibit A to exhibit B.
> Geronimo. Cochise. Sitting Bull.
> The battle is over. Only dull
> round of prison life (lost prairie).

Gould invokes a museum, archives, exhibits, all paracolonial artifacts that collect news of what "was freedom." In this thought experiment, the Dakota and Ho-Chunk and Sauk have been replaced, their prairies lost, picking up where the narrative on the Minnesota state seal will forever eventually end, beginning his booklength poem by accepting the predicate offered by the image on the old state seal ... before then almost breaking his own voice apart somehow, in a way I don't fully understand.

Most important, I think, is that Gould opens his book by speaking in an old-fashioned way, with a purposefully old-fashioned style of poetry, though neither mannered nor measured, befitting his station as a white writer from, as he puts it, "an old American family," speaking beautifully and calmly, weirdly and meditatively, and frankly madly, into the past, because that is where and how the settler colonial mindset has left the Native: in the past, on the flag, in the museum. How does a white writer write their way out of the past and into the real, when their subject is a violent and brutal nation that has historically preyed upon its own people, without first looking at and then beyond flags and vexillological narratives and beyond even the very history of literature itself and into the rivers and sorrows and sunsets of its many living people and its many beings and spirits seen and unseen, heard and unheard, felt and unfelt, written and unwritten, past and always present.

Gould with this book looks impossibly for a secret geometric doorway or spillway out of the smashed geography of the Mississippi watershed and its crushed archeology and literature ... and into a land and landscape that cannot be properly named or called in any European language: hence we read Gould pulling on multiple linguistic threads, trying to make the Dakota, Ojibwe, Sauk, French, Spanish, Hebrew, Egyptian, German, Russian, Greek, Old Norse, Aramaic threads speak with and inside an English that ranges from Shakespeare to Martin Luther King, and settles finally as an interlocutor with Black Elk and Mark Twain and Ophelia and Cleopatra, by setting in motion and both speaking to and ventriloquizing Christ, Mary the Mother of God, Benjamin Latrobe, the unnamed Ojibwe woman frozen in bronze at Itasca, as well as ancestral members of Gould's own family, all of it swirled together in great gusts of river water and barges full of mad song about and from and for the magi in Bethlehem to the quiet at Gettysburg and Antietam. This is a great poem on the order of Kamau Brathwaite's *Ancestors*, except this one is told in the white creole voice of those descended from the flag makers.

Gould tells us in his preface that he takes his title from the Eric Rohmer film "Le Rayon Vert," the green ray, whose final scene shows a couple sitting at the seaside watching the sun set over the water, and just before the sun disappears below the horizon it sends up one last parting ray, a green one, that ostensibly causes in the viewer, according to the 1882 Jules Verne novel of the same title, a momentary ability to see into their own heart and the hearts of others.

Thus Gould's book seems sandwiched between two sunset images. The red ray depicted on the old flag and invoked twice in Mary Eastman's poem and this one in Gould's:

> With a green flash, the last light rose
> from sunset. On the vertical,
> above the dark horizon
> like a wheat-blade – singular,
> enormous. Bleeding as the Delta flows
> widening on either side;
> melding in diapason
> *eleisons* of blue and red
> over the mud-green, violet furrows.

This is the green ray at sunset that Mary Henderson Eastman does not see. This is the green ray at sunset that coaxes our collective gaze from the flags and sunsets of the past back into our present heart lakes and language rivers. This is the green ray at sunset that replaces the French locution on the seal and flag "L'étoile du nord" with the Dakota phrase "Mni sóta makoce," makoce meaning homeland, mni water, sóta clear. And whoever speaks the history of this chain of sunsets that is Minnesota, that is the Mississippi watershed in particular and America in general, whoever speaks this or sings this as a song of balm against the silences of disregard and the flowing rivers of indifference, even in a white privileged creole voice, itself a colonized voice rising from a chorus of colonizing voices, we must realize that, if Benedict Anderson is right, it is precisely our literary workers and other language workers ("writers, teachers, pastors, lawyers," as Anderson says)[2] who are necessarily going to get this wrong.

This is not a history or a poem that anyone can get right. No one can. Because it is impossible to write a poem about America or from America that is not mad, or a poem about or from any nation qua nation, that does not silence as it speaks, that does not necessarily shove someone from its flags into the atmosphere. In the penultimate stanza of this poem Black Elk speaks, the Ojibwe woman in Itasca speaks, and Henry Gould speaks, as an alien at home on his flag, about looking into the heart of this serpent that we feed and from which we drink:

> In my mind I stand among low pine hills
> in the north country, looking south.
> A silver serpent
> shines in sunlight, bearing both
> wrath and hope. Earth-heart, that spills
> tears, water, blood.

– Gabriel Gudding
Normal, Illinois
May 19, 2024

---

[2] Anderson, Benedict. Imagined Communities: Reflections on the Origin and Spread of Nationalism. 76

OCTAVES

for Karen Donovan

1

They have gathered your feathers under glass.
Your arrowheads have become a collection.
What was freedom has evolved into. . . perfection.
Archives trace a cold trail (of wild grass).

I roam from exhibit A to exhibit B.
Geronimo. Cochise. Sitting Bull.
The battle is over. Only dull
round of prison life (lost prairie).

2

Tombstone epitaph.
Windblown wheat chaff.
Bones dry nearby,
beneath a vacant sky.

Tumbleweeds, dust bowl.
Roll along, film roll.
Cowboys, gallop on
into a rusted sun.

3

Oasis of resplendent pines,
gathering place of lost tribes,
home of broken hearts. . . your
lines betray the salt Caribs

and unremembered Africa. Shells,
uphold the barricade
and echo back your *ca-ri-ca*
until the sound return (as shade).

4

Is it the sea or is it a voice,
or is it a sea-voice (rocked
by heart-beats long-ago docked
in petrified wave-lengths, ice-

water)? Or the wind in a tree.
That one, rising like a broken delta.
Speaks through me.
Rafted away now. . . Huckleberry. *Selah*.

*

Cellular, turbulent, fluttering
fan of wings liquid in flight.
Fibrillated muttering
breaks open. Eyeing the daylight,

children. . . flow. Gather me out
now from immovable sacred stones
shattered against Cuzco mountains
(driftwood, echo, condor, shadow).

5   *J.C.*

Alabama. Trail
of summer.
Hail-
storm holiday. Drummer,

play slow. Taps. Blue.
Horn,
blow. Live again, re-
born.

6

Mississippi, Mississippi. . .
Gravel and silt slide down the stream.
Mississippi, Mississippi. . .
Spell it out, spell out your dream.

Why should I spell it out for you
(New York – D.C. – California)?
I hit the road before you do.
(Minnesota. . . Alabama. . .)

7

Where the twin empty railroad tracks
iron out the horizon (geometry
of a hobo wedding) the flickety flecks
of feathered circumstance might be

your guide. Might be.
Coyote pretends a plastic trance
for the tourists – then starts to dance. . .
and you remember. You're free (in memory).

4.1.97 *(April Fool's)*

I

1

Your birthday, J – it was just yesterday.
  And yet it seems an age ago.
    My limping memory
    has less and less each day to show.
  What can an old man do, but pray
for some kind of tender waterfall
– St. Anthony's, maybe? –
  of mercy... some *Deep River* squall.
  Afloat in a glide, across the Gulf... *M'aidez!*

Ancient familiar household things, handmade
  summon the pressure-chamber of the kiln.
    Mud-black, jungle green
    encircle the Spanish-Cretan bull.
  Proud head, flagged for the kill-parade –
arched back a Romano-Egyptian
mundus-mound. Some obscene
  scandal – Piero's premonition...
  Madonna del Parto, or *The Departure* (retrograde

Art Deco-Decadent). I don't know how
  to make this work, Asclepion.
    In the old room's high corner,
    near that torrid platter (Grecian)
  sits a quaint *Last Supper* (out of Mexico).
Is there eloquence in clay?
Mouths agape, poor mud-shapes holler
  collective joy – up to *That Day*
  (when *Rabbi* will rejoin us, here below).

And I have not spoken yet of the *Green Ray*.
  Le Rayon Vert. Some photons (bent,
    refracted through frigid glass
    of a Minneapolis evening) sent
  a parallactic element of the closing day

over the bull's-eye... over the heads
of lamb-chanting apostles,
    against a corner wall – dead
    center of this family history (*hallelujay*).

                                      2.1.23

                        2

    The music of what happens (*Luke* 2:22)
        when, at the corner of your eye
            light strikes to the heart
            from distant sun in the sky.
    When righteous Simeon cries *hallelu*
    and steadfast Anna still remains –
watches Simeon depart,
        notes the burbling Firstborn's
            first word : *sword* (searing even you).

                                      2.2.23

                        3

    With a green flash, the last light rose
        from sunset. On the vertical,
            above the dark horizon
            like a wheat-blade – singular,
        enormous. Bleeding as the Delta flows
    widening on either side;
melding in diapason
    eleisons of blue and red
        over the mud-green, violet furrows.

                                      2.4.23

4

A majestic Norway spruce outside the window
  stands like a foremast for the good ship
    Henry Duplex (310
    Cecil St.). Though the pilot slips
  sometimes into a daytime doze... lets go
the rudder, wheel. He's turning gray.
That mumbling Captain
 mirrors the river's skip-n'-sway –
   reverberates Time's pompous *diktat* (flow).

 Dreams at the oneness began. The wilderness.
   Over the Falls... where airborne fish
     cavort across moss-
     bound, glistening stones – where Finnish
   elk-milk merges with clouds, and bears press
  their noses against lichen boulder-
brothers. Paradise
 will nevermore get lost, grow older;
   thus were the Falls (St. Anthony's distress).

 But at St. Louis the course of this dream is run.
   That miserable *Geryon*
     whorls on his acid wings
   into whirlpools of *Phlegethon.*
   It is beneath the ice, a rancid undertone;
  the ceremony of destruction.
We had not seen such things
 unveiled, blind, bright Hyperion!
   – arcs of Black Rapids brazen the sun.

2.8.23

5

The river mirrors who we are (or were,
     just now). A gaudy circle, wobbling
          down the slope toward
          the Gulf. That terrifying goblin,
     child, is just a masquerade – the *Power*
of the Air is only air (waving
goodbye now, child).
     These proud, sulfurous, misbehaving
          ne'er-do-wells flit past their passing hour.

     That startling tall 19th-century photo
          of *Jessie Ophelia* (granddaughter
               of Jackson and Susan
               Quick – my great-grandmother)
     sheds rays around some cryptic studio.
     Her *fin-de-siècle* finery,
pre-Raphaelite fan –
     beneath the lunar mystery
          of a wide black hat, her dark eyes glow.

     Grandfather Jackson was a river-pilot
          on the Mississippi. He died
               young, aboard a Union
               hospital ship (somewhere outside
     Vicksburg). *Sound – mark twain.* The plot
     thickens. Churns (turbid, dangerous).
Three, two... one.
     No man's an island! hollers
          Lady Day – *Nazir.* Singe the knot.

                                        2.9.23

6

The river hosts a multitude of schools
  of fish, and fishermen... of creatures
    known and unknown, great
    and small. That clan of clever painters
  of the *Cubist School* (Parisian) flouted rules
 of both decorum and timespace
on behalf of their innate
 vivacité – discounted grace
   of *jeux d'esprit* (playful *trompe l'oeils*).

 I wanted to reach out and touch the bird,
   it seemed so real. Mary Lincoln
     (legend states) fainted
     on seeing the portrait of the *Man*
  Who Died (Ford's Theatre); *only say the word*
 and I will raise him from the dead.
Rendered full color – painted
  smiling, 9 feet tall (instead
    of Brady *rigor mortis*). Wry, he murmured

  something hardly anybody heard.
    A private witticism, maybe –
      yet it carried far
      across that paralytic sea
   of wounded faces. Suddenly, absurd
  and hopeless anguish, suffering,
all casualties of war
  assumed some *habitus* of meaning –
    Lincoln's carrier-pigeon wings... whirred.

  My brother Jim, just recovered from covid
    called to tell me he had found
      important information
     on the family. Some newshound
   in New Orleans (1877) described a huge *Testudinid*

17

(a green sea turtle, 7,332 pounds)
shipped to E.M. Friedheim
(*née* Elizabeth Quick) in St. Louis...
a sea-gift, via *Pettizrem*. Open the lid!

2.11.23

7

Old sap still seeps from the lofty pine
    standing so upright and green
        at the prow of the house.
    All the slow changes, seen
    leaning into the buffeting winds... a fine
sand, in its diffident hourglass
scraping smooth time's loss
    – like that brown circle of needles
        molding your footstone, O steadfast one.

The stars are so bright tonight. There's *Orion*,
    there's the *Big Bear*. Somewhere
        I think there's a poetry
        young, fiery and spruce as you are,
    Tree – you straight aspiring spire of green!
    A tree that will not die, but shines
like a lighthouse in the sky.
    The heart of all the valentines –
        Who, from the galaxies, murmurs : *Be Mine.*

2.13.23

8

Your little boat glides down the mighty river,
  your canoe, your wooden mandorla,
    your Viking ship, your casket.
    Moses was lifted, *au-delà*
  so gently... *may my baby never shiver*
 so, but rest him in my bosom –
Lord, I ask it –
 so my beseeching brook may come
    to mirror Thee; thine orphan child deliver.

I remember Tibetan monks in Providence
  sifting their dazzling mandalas
    (ephemeral sand, wind)
    along old New England river-plazas –
  to memorialize a molten coincidence
 of fire and water, earth and air.
So the river quickened
  with symmetrical formations there;
    so Time eddied round one's *Reminiscences*

of 1865. The still-life, the *trompe-l'oeil*
  play *jeux d'esprit*, mind-games
    with your imagination;
    so this river's history defames –
  swerves between mirrored sky and rancid oil
until a fraudulent *Manco Capac*
leaps up, and your attention
  (mesmerized) is *all compact*...
    so the bold evil stirs, brings hell to boil.

And yet... I say, the *Galilee of the Nations*
  began beside a mountain spring
    in the woods – where water
    first emerged, clear, burbling
  like a child. And the *mandala of the Magdalen*

arose near Magdala, beside the sea;
a round perimeter
  of rosy fire. It was the flame, *To Be* –
    the fiddlehead furnace (green heart's foundation).

2.14.23

9

The poem drops everything, leaves home,
  lights out for the territory.
    Lopes along the river
  looking for Hobo Hideaway,
where slow smoke-fumes meander some
athwart the river's sinuous wisdom –
relentless palaver
  drafting the children of the Kingdom
    nearer to Thy salt-blue, sharkfin tomb.

2.15.23

10

My tugboat *Henry Duplex* chugs along
  stubborn as that Sea Scout
    vessel, *Pegasus*,
  in 1940 (coming about
  in the archival photo). Nine sea lads strong
standing at attention there
mirrored on calm surface
  upside down – under the river;
    Pegasus a seahorse now (with dolphin-gong).

We're swimming underwater, gurgling
  incomprehensible slogans.

20

That green, refracted ray
  descends from elsewhere – *Son of Man's*
  wing-lamp. Light's word, swift… burgling
the sandy shore, from Lake Itasca
to the Delta. All the way.
 Sea Scouts bore his body (*wei la la*)
  to feverish Biloxi, Benjamin (you, following).

 I think about that architect, Latrobe.
  Emigrating from England, to design
   the Capitol building.
  I think about another sign,
  the river's sign of otherness – this *Globe*
where Shakespeare carried out
the bodies (laughing, crying)
 aboard an allegorical paddleboat.
  Jack Quick's, Jessie Ophelia's. Rend, robe.

2.18.23

11
i.m. John Berryman

This morning Sunday quiet, broken by sirens.
  Looked out to see 10 vehicles
   (police, fire, EMS)
  convened over the riverbank's
 ravine. I ask a fireman. *Someone*
slipped through the ice, he said.
He's in the ambulance.
 And I reckoned that poet much-maligned
  who faced this frozen river all alone.

 He fell into steep snow, near St. Anthony Falls.
  You build the house, Lord, *with*
   what lumber you have.
  He left us his rusted green scythe

21

of hope vs. hope, of grace and miracles
out of tune with the world – but not
with *You*. That shining wave
of steel, above your *Rio's* heart
glints with lambent fusion of good wills.

2.19.2

12

Small things intrigue me now, as I've become
smaller – the *Brain Science Center*
across the street might take
an interest, some century.
And since St. Paul's is smaller than that dome
in Rome, state capitols are
lesser forms of magic –
size is everything, in war.
An acorn is a coracle in your green kingdom.

There was a congregation of live voices
in the limbs, a happy gathering;
woodpeckers, ravens, doves
within their conclave (tree-ring
twirling wave of blue-green spruces,
aquamarine). Unswayed by that
remover, who removes
like a tugboat stuck on Ararat
after the Flood... still swanning deuces.

3.1.23

13

A full moon floats over Minneapolis
  as it did 5000 years ago
   over the Nile. Isis
  searches for Osiris, now
and on the Mississippi. What is this,

  anyhow? The monarch in his moon-boat
 sails upstream, in a river-dream;
Earth, from her green axis
 emits a ray, a clay light-beam.
  Notre Dame exhales (one solemn note).

  The light shines in the darkness, and the darkness
   has not overcome it. Manko
    shuffles a deck, on deck...
   all is silence, river-flow.
  A human silhouette stands motionless
 and resolute, athwart the prow
(Monitor, Merrimack);
 the sparklers begin to glow
  and now the battle's on (*woe to Osiris*).

                    3.6.23

14

I walked along the steep snowbound ravine
  above the river, on Spring's first day.
   I heard a soft sound
   little waterfalls, washing away
downstream   fusing a kind of unison

(an undertone). The Iraq War began
 two decades ago. I was
one of the hawks, then –
 part of the violence... because
  I couldn't face another Vietnam! *Atone,*

Hobo, for hollowness, if you can –
 serpentine Geryon flaunts the shiny
   face of a righteous man.
  Our confidential destiny
 drifts downward, on rungs of treason
and a turtledove croons anxiously
over this cardboard Roman
 ampitheatre – where we play
  out our hypocrisies across a wooden

X or *O* (the red of wrath, the blue
 of woe). It is a tightly-woven
   tapestry... so fine,
  so cunning, there is no one
 so wise as to discern its pattern (only you).
 Only water, in this world
is able to combine
 clarity and movement, whorled (pearled).
  Come down to the *Rio*, Johnny, now...

and be renewed.

3.20.23

15

The first sign of spring, in these latitudes
   is light itself, growing stronger.
     After the long winter
    my own shadow grows... longer.
  Life's a correlation of small fortitudes.
 The little birds are still alive;
the rabbit-bitten, bitter
 shrub might put forth leaf
   again... (O tiny bronze beatitudes).

  I visit St. Paul every day.
    Only a block away, just past
     the Brain Science Center.
    Yet it's a mystery (on the *Last*
  Day) to me : how it might be. To die
 yet not to die – to be reborn;
my body (disinterred
 anew) a desiccated corn
   of oak, turned green... a King of May?

  I know a man, who was rapt up
   to the third heaven, he wrote. We are
    all blind, regarding that.
    My Providence is subtler
   than every serpent... canst thou drink my cup?
  The undulating river flows,
a sword, green-rusted
 through this land of mocking crows.
   I dream a *Union* (yonder, beyond Devil's Gap).

3.27.23

16

God gave me this tough painted carapace –
  or did I manufacture it
    myself? *Isolato*,
    chilly bachelor, squat
  lumberer, devoid of winged grace
 or generosity! No fellow-
feeling – only the slow
 and stubborn will to go,
    to go… at my own muddy river-pace.

  Whole civilizations build upon my back
    built like a tank. I am their stony
      ego-idiot, their unknown
    grunt, buried sans ceremony.
   And all my dreams enmesh in this mosaic
   that floats upon my curvature –
Ricardian dome of bone
  mounted on coppery substructure
    (my plastron, like the platform pharaohs make).

  I am paradigm of all the immobile-
    portable homes in the cosmos.
      When Mrs. Elizabeth Quick-
    Friedheim of fair St. Louis
   hauled up one of my deep-water people
 in chains from seedy New Orleans,
anon the sea-salt flick
 of her blood-reds and ultramarines
    would pen the spines of slave-barrack and steeple.

  So in the noise of air above water
    we lose the soft flute-sound
      of dawning, baby Spring.
    And in the maze of square and round
   every turtle is an einstein (*solitaire*

center of some unrepeatable
design). The hat in the ring
  resembles your turtle, too – mobile
    wing of one lost gray, lost flicker.

    Lost son, lost daughter. So daub your shell,
      grandfather, grandmother – paint
        us a masquerade (so red,
        so blue). Turn the invidious complaint
      into Bosch Monitor, from depth of hell.
    Into a Bruegel Merrimack
for Mardi Gras... dead
  center of irenic turtle-back,
    Cahokian matrix (whence visions well).

3.30.23

17

The river has a lizard-look, today.
 Her steel of gray-green-brown
  slides by (so smooth,
  so dangerous). *Goin' down*
 to China... have a good time. May
 still far off – the snow half-melted
in these parts, forsooth.
 When that Aprill with her show'rs pelted
  the sodden ground... potholes... thus my *Lay*

 of Minneapolis (the weather report).
  But every river's source, the heart,
   cannot be plumbed (*mark*
   twain) so easily – each chart,
  each horoscope, floats off. Ask Mort :
 he's no longer with us. Flimsy
the craft, the feral shark
 is furious. There is a time for whimsy
  and a time for grief – life sells you short,

  Abe Lincoln, MLK. Yet in that market,
   anyway, you played no part
    (JFK was there
   also). Blithe innocent heart...
  still girl... the husbandman is quiet,
 just as you. It is a kindness
at the root of things, bare
 mercy, out of great distress.
  Slow river-mystery (so deep, so great).

4.3.2

18

Rough drafts of spring, mud-sloppy
   rehearsals, tentative runs of green
      under blind cold mounds
     of reactionary snow. The scene
  (a leftover lotus-flower, sleepy poppy)
 demands a do-over. Owls hoot;
sculls, megaphones
 vibrate through thawed-out
   Father-of-Waters (slow-seething Pappy).

And way down yonder, beyond many unseen
snake-bit
   bends, far echoes emanate...
    evening hilarity
   aboard the *Delta Queen* (late
  of St. Lou – bound for N'Orleans retrofit).
 They're playing Shakespeare tonight
(creaky gratuity);
 I wouldna pay for a pistol fight
  between two pigeons, quoth the Fat Knight.

Reverb of river ripples aslant the bow
   on either side... thus words echo
    in your sleepy mind,
   Horatio. *Ophelia's no mo.*
 The trip's end is like this, somehow.
 By the time you reach the wharves
the whole river's behind
 you – like the jagged swerves
  of a broken heart (clay cracked by plow).

4.6.23

19

These bony April branches will be budding
before long. Each rackety tree
a kind of wooden river,
urging its wide delta (slowly,
relentlessly) into the sky – flooding
the Milky Way with rivulets
that fade and disappear
beneath a stream of stars... motes
alight on blue-black *Ocean River* (brooding).

And the great dark-green delta of the oak
whispers through its summer leaves
back toward its future ground.
Grass destination none conceives,
until an old word (*rood*) is uttered – spoke
on the ashen wheel of Yggdrasil.
You build your house atop that mound
of Golgotha – *place of the skull*;
on your adamant frame the world-wave broke.

Once upon a time, that other Henry
strove with all his schoolcraft toward
true headwaters – a clear spring
of water, buried in the wood.
Discovering only one bright copper penny –
emblem of that massive brazen
Ouroboros times shall bring.
And *may the circle be unbroken*...
history wheeling on that crown (uncanny).

4.7.23

20

To build a faery-boat of dew, or tears;
  to go slipping down the branches
    of the tree of life;
  to see how the river quenches
  herself in a fiery dusk of sea-roses,
 out into her infinite delta,
like the azure wife
 of a setting sun (with a last tattoo
   of ocean waves, drumming the sandbars).

These pink clouds at sunset, a memory
  of the sea. Memory like a grain
    of salt – like a gyroscope
  in the marrow. It was the Magdalen
  whose crumb of memory would magnify
  the loaf of Peter and of Paul –
when her grief-stricken hope
 against hope would make the Rabbi whole
   again (bright gardener in the cemetery).

Wisdom lurks hidden in our recollection,
  Plato's Socrates insisted.
    Deceitful and corrupt
    above all things, Jeremiah countered,
  is the heart. We learn to our destruction
  how malignity and treason
from our own heartland erupt;
  we must recall a Lincoln lesson.
    Our forsaken UNION *is Love's benediction.*

4.8.23

21

This lambent milky air of early April
 on a quiet peaceful Sabbath day.
　At Appomattox once
　you brought the dogs of war to bay,
　U.S. – if only they would just keep still!
 Humans, shackled by mortality
envy the insolence
 of gods – so our mentality
　mimes demons. *O deliver us from evil.*

　One bright copper penny glimmered, once
　　beneath the shadows of a well
　　 like throne, or platform.
　　Your prophets muttered out of hell
　of righteousness – a name for innocence;
 it was their cycloid whorls of sorrow
made cosmos grow warm
 and personal. It was tomorrow
　borne from such deracinated happenstance.

　Very personal. Beaming, spewing
　across scripture, verbiage.
　　Unpredictable rumor
　of a new *Aeon* (shuddering Mage
　out of Persepolis, mayhap?) – revising
 fixed ambivalence of gods and men,
so that divine humor
 anoints a Child… wrath-driven
　Servant (cosmic AGAPE imbuing).

4.9.23

22

The dark river is out there tonight. Across
  the street. Remorseless, at the nadir
    of two steep ravines;
    a brazen serpent, under your radar.
  She is your time – bearing grief and loss
 on rickety raft, on frail canoe.
Don't ask what it means;
 we are molded by her current too
   (ferns field Black Elk's testament of moss).

  The river mirrors, mirrors. All those
   tall tales you read in high school
     imbibed on your mother's lap
    merge (in ambiguous, whirlpool-
   poem). Compendium of otherness.
  Childhood, you know, Ramon Fernandez,
is like that – the trap
 for a catfish catches us.
   Elusive (nested deeper than Loch Ness).

  Yet this sweet night air floats over water
   like another stream, on another plane;
    like scent of far-off summer
    (something no one can explain).
  Memories run deep. Your son, your daughter
 (you). I would paddle to the source
if I were Black Elk's drummer –
 leap upon his snow-white horse
   blessed by blazing dawn… (hum, river-mutter).

                                              4.12.23

23

Jonah, tossed unceremoniously
  off the steamboat, was swallowed up
    by a giant catfish.
    Or was it a snapping turtle? Sup
  for a river monster, churning to the sea.
Within that fetid, mud-caked cavern
America was the wish
 of desperate, inverted children –
  dream, dear fiction-spun Reality!

  We had to rework the lingo in order to meet
    the outright immensity of it all.
      The old bimetallic crown
    of ruddy gold, the great chant royal
  molts to kaleidoscopic *Paraclete* –
the twangs and swerves of immigrants
(jay-haunted pine).
 So this valve of Mississippi currents
  squares them all to one cycloid quartet.

  Waves, here, roll not to the shore
    but to the sea. *From sea to sea.*
      That Ocean in your eye
    only an infant memory,
    small as a tear. (All this happened before.)
  And the Paraclete's a radiant cloud
in the shape of *Columbia* –
 a curve of wings, in the Lydian mode.
  Two wings... six arrows (Arkadian score).

                  4.14.23

24

A single mote of brazen light reflects
   the sun, from muddy river murk.
     One *aw-shucks* craggy face
    you know – from Plains, or Keokuk.
   The *People's Choice*… a penny resurrects
  sometimes. Out of the turbid sludge
of sad, hard-bitten hearts –
 of willful ignorance (mean grudge
   of US); that hatred one soft word deflects.

   Flutes and trumpets of the woodland nymphs
    lift through the branches of the stream.
     It is a wooded river-
    current, slow – unmoved by scheme
   or demagogue's design (those shady triumphs
  of *tromp-l'oeil*, the metamorphoses
of guile, the whole quiver
 of malice… all its poisoned arrows).
   Lightning in that oak makes emerald lamps.

   The arc of history is long, but it bends
    toward justice. *Come, drink wisdom*
     from my breast, she sings.
    The *milk-&-honey* of this plumb-
   bob *mark-twain* tree's eternal friends
  rings – lopes along – a platform,
or a stage for kings…
 its *Globe* a Thames-borne river-dome
   or acorn-coracle (rounding our ends).

                     4.17.23

25

Lightning and thunder play in this April murk.
  They boom, they flash their monitory
    ammunition. It is
    the Minotaur of spring, angry
  at ice-manacles – his bullhorn spark.
 Cat hides under dinner table.
In Lisbon and Cadiz,
  the guts of the guitar (if you are able)
    prong through silence. Etch their mark.

  Down there in the dark V of the ravine
    the river churns to flood. Span
      this, if you can,
      Roebling, Eads... *the Son of Man*
    is born of woman – in her blood and pain.
   So the waters roar together
(Abyssinian
  vortex) – hypnotic tether
    of one fey Dvorak nymph (Victorian).

  The whispers came through a rug backdrop,
    on your paddleboat stage.
      Was it thee, Ophelia?
    Cleopatra, Desdemona? *Age*
    had brought me to the sea (big turtles flop
   into that hardpan stream). Gold
on your brow, Kythira –
  gift from *maudit* Richard 3rd?
    Climbs from the parking lot (rebukes the *scop*).

4.19.23

26

Life exults in waves, in wave-forms.
  The enormous fish was a submarine
   for Jonah (still pulsing,
    underwater). Points on a screen
  mark a frail constellation (driven by storms).
 The search for God is a human thing
(very). So let us sing
 that ineffable *Person*, at end of the string
  of sense (our personal cat's-cradle, charms).

 Jo-Jo (*Giuseppe-Jonah*), in the '20s
  felt himself a remnant (scrap
   of paper, horseshoe).
  Warbled through his dented pipe
 of a *salience* (air-bubble, in a carpenter's
 gold level). Incandescent foam
of apotheosis – for you
 and for me. When we come home
  to that well-loved cosmos (*dove-syestra-brooders*).

 A small green acorn floated down the stream.
  It was an elf, or it was Frisbee
   (or it was a Selkie,
  maybe); a crown of charity,
  little ones, for a milkman (an American dream).
 The sea-salt waited for her
on a wave of humility.
 A cello droned across the floor
  of Ocean River – spun one Memphis diadem.

4.20.23

27

Conscience is intangible light – a feather
  on a green radius, from heart
    to mind. Weightless
      itself, yet you can build on it –
    tall pine in Lebanon, its aerial tether.
  The lid upon Lod, Diospolis
is lifted up by grace,
  walking his casket on St. George's
    Day (that unknown soldier... fleet bellwether).

  This fortitude of April sun's our good,
    in northern latitudes. Our *Son*
      of Man, our Everyman –
    like *Manco Capac*, to the perihelion
  he vaults. No sign of serpentine falsehood;
    his effulgent gold doubloon
will imprint your schoolcrafted skin
  like flattery of a bright balloon.
    He will reward you with the coin of fraud.

  The measure you measure shall be measured unto
you.
    UNION = EQUALITY = CONNECTION :
      these three are one
    propounded Thierry (a theologian
  at Chartres). Mayhap the river forms an oxbow
  there? Mercurial excerpt
of circumference... (someone
  unknown)? Black Elk is plumb (curt).
    Black, Green... Red, Yellow, Blue.

                                        4.23.23

28

The stream arose out of the womb of spring
  like a signal from a continent
    of pristine otherness.
  What the *Paraclete* meant
  about that *Son of Man* Mary would bring :
 He will take the clear and fluid form
of one meant for service.
 You will only belatedly behold him
   in the tracks he leaves (of love, of suffering).

  The tragedies of politics in every age
    are forecast by each quiet child.
      Remembering a past
    already lost (gone misty, wild).
   Aye there's the rub, for all that surly rage.
  We carpenter our lives together
out of this forest – here
  the only king is the king of weather.
    Noah (still working at the steamboat stage).

  Young Benjamin Latrobe and Robert Fulton
    made that effort, on the Ohio –
      and failed. It doesn't matter.
    Behind Latrobe's labyrinthine brow
   lurked an artful sense, a Greek ambition
  (conceived in LIBERTY... dedicated
to EQUALITY... that higher
  LAW). So *Love* is predicated,
    hums yon changeable dove (Columbian).

4.24.23

29

What will they play on the riverboat tonight?
  Richard the III? In the distance there
    a yodeling family hubbub
   busy with living – pretty bare
  and improvised. The river's a kind of boat
 herself, passing through St. Louis
on a round balsa bubble.
  Where I found *Jessie Ophelia Lawrence* –
  grandchild of *Andrew Jackson Quick*, pilot –

  on an old handwritten family tree. Drawn up
   by my own great-granddad, *George* –
    Jessie's husband – upstream
   in Minneapolis. By the only gorge
  on the whole *Rio del Espiritu* (yup -
St. Anthony Falls). Where they lived and grew
long ago, in a dream
  down the River Road from here (*Soo
   Line*). On a raft of violets, rue, and hyssop

  too, Ophelia (your beautiful dark eyes,
   shaded by wide-brimmed hat
    in the old photograph).
   The play's the thing, dark heart
  that lifts you to the surface – in disguise.
 A camouflage of river-tears;
light far-off laugh
 afloat above these churning years.
  The ship cleaves toward remote night skies.

4.26.23

30

The river breaks just once – at the Falls
    in Minneapolis. On its way
     to St. Paul. Twin
    Cities, Cities of the Twin... *ey?*
   Man is a poet, and her myths build walls –
  break walls. First Man
was *Ymir*, they
 say – was "his own twin" –
   hermaphrodite. Of his clay the gods made meals.

   Of Their flesh the gods made earth and sky
    (the poor lumbering clay-wight).
     It was the first divide
    (post that primordial slight
   of twin from twin); so mortal beings die
  as well, along with fader-mutter
Ymir. None can hide
 from the bare facts – this sputter
   of violence, these unjust motors. *Why,*

   O why? Job pleads to Jove. Moreover
    money backtalks everything
     rejoins Ecclesiastes.
    Socialism for the rich, cries King
   and rugged capitalism for the poor,
  that's the trouble. Give me the man
not passion's slave (sez
 Hamlet) – there be the woman
   after mine own heart (*Ophelia-flower*).

   St. Paul and Minneapolis... the Jew
    and the Greek, the Roman Catholic
     and the Protestant, Faith
    and Reason, Red and Blue... sick
   partisan... healthy ideologue... you

know what kind of shape I'm in,
Big Muddy. A gaping mouth,
  down to *Ginnunga Gap* – sin
    swallows me like *Jason Joan* (in a rearview

    mirror). *I'm a Manu*, said the Indian;
      but you don't know. Where's the boat,
      Jason, Jonah? The canoe?
      Our balance, rectitude... afloat –
    like that gold bubble of air at the median
  of a carpenter's wooden yardstick;
like a casket of yew
  become stone *trompe-l'oeil*... eucharistic
    Grail. A Lincoln log (Sole-Human).

4.30.23

31

The mind of the river foresees its final end
   in an azure transfiguration
    a neverending dance
   of shimmering, post-riverine
  diaphanous waves. It is the way we bend
 to ineluctable telos
an implacable persistence
 offering force an answering force
  molding a buoyant firmness out of sand.

  That man on his cross, at the end of his road
   his arms forced up toward the sky
    shapes a like denouement
   lifts an ensign in the eye
  of Everywoman, Everyman... whence flowed
 each bitter human memory
each salt monument
 that swims into eternity
  (*Rio del Espiritu Santo*, in delta mode).

  So imagination shapes our ocean grave
   and lifts us to its hovering
    aerie – an eagle's nest
   of innocence. For souls... ringing
  one pine-green mast, one Mayday stave
 for every Jessie and Ophelia
blithe, sprightly, blest
 skipping around their Milky Way –
  Hamlet the May King's crown (transparent wave).

5.1.23

32

Ophelia in the stream-bed, with her tangled
   wreath of herbs and wildflowers.
    A mournful Queen of May
    faintly singing of the mowers,
   as she sinks downstream... broken, heart-mangled.
  Hamlet has lost the name of action.
Pale-faced, scholarly,
 he waits on the usurper's con –
   a *trompe-l'oeil* of the human (fanged, new-fangled).

   The river is addictive (much like song).
    There is a danger in that weird
     undertow of whorls,
    its soporific current – glide
   thee who dare! Only the constant prong
  of upright steersmate will remain
afloat upon these squalls –
  scrolling their surf, hoisting disdain
   for anonymous fishermen (enforcing wrong).

   Likewise Latrobe, ineffable architect
    of Capitol dome, built paddle-boats –
    tracked his own son
    to New Orleans. Where the Fates
   (weird sisters) raveled their Voodoo dialect
  with scarlet fever – to the grave
(for both). Sun-Charon
  oars libations there... a wave
   of honeygold mead (penny for the elect).

5.5.23

33

The proud river moves with stupefying force –
    blinding, mesmerizing. Drowning,
      sometimes. *Élan vital*
    of a continent... disowning
  stasis, always – flushing junkyard remorse
 into the azure trash bin of the sea.
Seagulls, that's all.
  Shrimp traps (a Cajun mystery).
    The histrionic Duke hollers, *A horse!*

  My kingdom for a horse! – across the boards
    of his homemade (borrowed) flatboat.
      Ophelia remains
      tracing a circle, still afloat;
    Hamlet will be tripping aft, backwards
  to the wheelhouse... where Cap
negotiates the lanes
  of muddy boils (a bloody mishap).
    Uneasy rides the prow, upon such river-surds.

  And you hear the long-drawn note of the milk train
    in the early morning, in Arkansas
      maybe – one solitary
      lonesome hoot. And you know it was
    in drowsy Memphis once, downstream, where the
pain
  came to a head; where the King
foresaw his ordinary
  sacrifice. And you hear everything
    again (the minor key, the Jordan-flow, the rain).

5.7.23

34

The *May King* burns with righteous indignation
   like Cú Chulainn, or Ezekiel,
     fiery John the Baptist.
    By the rivers of Babylon, or Hell
   we hung up our harps – O wayward nation!
   How like an anxious mother hen
I cajoled thee to my nest...
  and thou wouldst not! Haste then
   to Gehenna, ye pernicious shepherds! Begone!

   The *May King* sleeps in his long canoe... Osiris
    in the river silt. Forgotten –
     like those twin redheads
    in the Irish legend. Fated men,
     doomed to walk the American night (endless).
   River-maidens ravel garlands
round that woe-tempered
  touchpiece... for treasonous brigands;
   a penny in a dragon's mouth (at Inverness

   or Appomattox). *With malice toward none,*
   with charity for all... here
    plumbed a true republican;
   for that *liberty* we bought so dear
  was planted first in *love of neighbor*, hon.
  The war you reap in fields of Mammon
is not about religion
  but rather spite, money, dominion –
   you do not know Me, spake the Son of Man.

                 5.8.23

35

I'm old enough to remember the slow-rolling saga
   of sun-bleached *Burma-Shave* billboards
    like the intermittent flash
    of a funny lighthouse... for bored
   kids on endless summer drives (going gaga).
  We, the Sign-Making Animal
out of obscure mish-mash
 find means to say, *all shall be well* –
   the denouement of all our illness, Gonzaga.

   St. Louis (where the Sea-Turtle came)
    suffers from chaos and injustice,
     like most places. Yet
    I am moved by the catenary sweetness
   of that sea-bright steel Archway (its sturdy frame).
  The river is a sullen monster
sometimes – that's what
 life is. A challenge to St. George (or
  Georgia). History's a gaudy chess game

  for the child, pure in heart. American dream.
   The government shall be upon
    his shoulder, Magdalen.
   That trashman in Memphis is the *Son*
 of Man. Black Elk's eagle is supreme
 in these badlands, my friend
(six-sided, crystalline
 and burning star). *This is the end*,
  America. Hexagonal night (of milky cream).

5.12.23

36

i.m. Jonathan Raban

You wanted to skip with Huck into the wilderness
  atop the mesmerizing, mighty stream
    apart from *all people*,
  intrepid Jonathan. Your trireme
a frail aluminum fishing boat (stressed
by that relentless river-flow).
Yet rescue was personal –
  a tough lockmaster you didn't know
  your *Father of Waters* (gave you saving advice).

And on your way to the Delta, you encountered
  you got to know, personally
    some ornery worn-down folk
  of American back country
– all their lonesome, impeccable, plain weird
recalcitrance. And then, in Memphis
a branch of MLK
  (Judge Otis Higgs) bore you his witness –
  a wedding in Cana (*Equality* = carpenter's *Word*).

Your reached the delta exhausted to the bone.
  The symphonic serpent merged into
    another magnitude,
  a greater immensity. Here, too
came Benjamin Latrobe, on a quest of his own –
beneath tomb-shade of his well-loved son
he sketched a certitude
  of wave-forms, domes... the diapason
  of benign creation. *Coracles* (divine/human).

5.14.23

37

You snake down Mississippi's crooked spine,
　　you're like to see occasions strange.
　　　There be but one sin
　　　unforgivable across the Grange
　　declared the *Son of Man* – know what I mean?
　　How these men can glorify sweet Jesus
Lord, bring thy Kingdom in
　while spewing hatred, rage and malice
　　at *those others*... is this not the Spirit's treason?

　　They are hypocrites. Their gods are Mammon
　　　and proud Moloch. Humble charity
　　　　is unknown territory
　　　to such hearts of mean asperity.
　　And like a drop of poison, evil will soon
　devour minds in fanatic madness...
shrivel generosity
　the prime simplicity of kindness
　　with suffocating hatred – pure suspicion.

　　Here, in May-time Minneapolis
　　　were moments of stillness, quiet peace;
　　　　sunlight; the scented
　　　avalanches of crabapple trees.
　　We say to the ravaged land, *come back to this.*
　　Benjamin Latrobe would weep
for the bartered dome
　of his wisdom; for the delicate sweep
　　of Liberty's design – mercy and justice.

5.16.23

38

If we think : the river is a sign for Time.
 If we think : the river is unceasing,
  ineluctable. And think
  the tiny branchlets of my being
 wind their way around a heart (prime
suspect). I search my memory.
She whispers – *Eat, drink.*
 American recovery
  might be the matter of a simple rhyme.

This is no laughing matter, noble Henry.
 You've walked the edge of the frozen bridge
  time out of broken mind
  and if there were no simple courage
 none would recall their perfidy, their glory.
 Man was put upon this earth
for one thing only. Kind
 is the grave for the unknown, simple serf;
  for the innocent child, whose grace is poverty.

Pindar walked his dance-steps, with nimble care.
 For the heroes of the commonweal
  there's final elegance
  in martyrdom – that last appeal
 to the *Father in heaven* (house of the stare).
 The river's angry with America.
Yet beneath her immense
 St. Louis futility, floats the arcana
  of the canoe (*mandorla* of Railsplitter).

5.21.23

39

Latrobe, Benjamin. From whose cranium
  emerged the U.S. Capitol dome
   like Athena from Athens.
   Plied the Mississippi chrome,
  old New Orleans... went to his long home
there (just like his son – fever).
How you proceed depends
 upon your glass, Shakespeare.
  Your compass. What is Man, compared to Rome?

  Serene late May in Minneapolis
   after the snow and ice are gone
    almost like Paradise.
   A dream within a dream, Jordan
  within another dream, my dear Alice
(so curious). If the *Son of Man*
didn't actually rise
 from the dead, yet his Word did – and
  between Word and Person is only a kiss.

  You can't comprehend what I'm trying to say.
   That's okay... I can't either.
    This fabric of our dream
   is frail, sighed Prospero/Shakespeare;
  the Mississippi flows to Memorial Day.
  Time guides us toward the ghosts
to reconcile us with them;
 after all, they were our hosts.
  Itasca springs rip their melodious way.

       5.27.23

40

Have you seen the river's quick folds and eddies
   turning, tumbling so smoothly
      like the *Rainbow Portrait*
      of that ineffable *Queen of Faery* –
   intelligence of eyes and ears... silk mercies,
lizard mercilessness? *O*
Ouroboros – Fate
   and Fortune intertwined! Let's go
      discover where the fetid serpent lies.

   Was it Heraclitus who opined, *Reality*
      is a child building sandcastles
         (– or something like that)?
      Or is it like, when Jacob wrestles
   with Angel, he wins – by way of disability?
   History is a slanting top;
and out of this oven-planet
   of a kiln, spins a marble... a copper
      penny... twirling like a gyroscope. *To be*

   or not to be, mutters the Prince of sorrows.
      Of sparrows. *There is a Providence,*
         and its name is : *glorious*
         abasement. I give in evidence
      John Kennedy, of scattered brain-roses;
   I give the milk-&-honey bravery
of MLK; I kiss
   the spinning penny of grey-
      hearted Abraham (love's *wheels-within-wheels*).

5.30.23

41

The wellsprings of childhood we hardly remember.
  Your font of equilibrium.
    Hidden Irvine Park
  with its great oaks, lilacs in bloom –
its tall black-iron Parisian fountain. Whisper
of calm summer rain, Marcel
on which you embark
 into a Mississippi whorl...
  Degas in New Orleans. Upstream, *mon frère.*

  Calme, luxe. The river of lost time.
    History turns on its oar
      (on your pilot ear).
    Mémoire of what came before
    (entering the whirlpool). Crime
  against the child you were. Remorse.
love casts out fear
  Mercy. *The arc of the universe
  is long*... its far sea-bell is in memoriam.

  I think of the tree-rings of these oaks
    in Irvine Park. Imagine an acorn
      like a coracle.
    Fold out of fold is being born
  slowly, invisibly... green spokes
on a wheel of kingdoms. America
in a Lincoln oracle
 is my Memorial Day; this bull's-eye
  in the theatre – no betrayal revokes.

5.31.23

42

Ol' Man River. To think of Mississippi
  as an open wound. Out of the heartland,
    Time's blood and water.
    Like someone robbed of a natural end,
  before their time. Cut off, prematurely.
  Taken away by violence.
O planetary mutter,
  undertone of woeful grievance...
    who will restore the shattered hero of clay?

    I see these curving folds, these riverbank ridges –
    like clay wave-forms around a wound.
      Set firm in time-space.
      Immoveable against the surround
  of vast entropic Ocean (whence all emerges).
  The wound is pride. A wolfish
urge to destroy, deface –
  since before the age of Gilgamesh
    a glove thrown down against kindness and peace.

    Flint and water, water and flint... Joseph
    lifted his cup toward brotherly
      envy, and forgave them all.
    And so the ark floated buoyantly
  again – across its wine-dark sea (bright *nef*).
  Civilization is mercy,
sweet lovingkindness.
  Overcoming adversity –
    where Ocean curves her catenary staff.

6.3.23

43

Moses, rocking in his reed-cradle, grew slowly
　　as a child, spoke slowly (speech
　　　impediment). His people
　　spread like pebbles on a beach
　grew slowly too, spoke haltingly – rarely.
　Terse proverbs, thrown like nails
against wood, were staple.
　The world is a battle. Who prevails
　depends upon the notching of a tally.

　Then something happened no one could explain.
　　But the charisma of that prophet
　　　came from a *chrism*, poured
　　over his head, by *J*... out
　of the River *J*. It was like a kind of rain
　from clouds overhead... soft and grey
as turtledove, from a gourd
　like a turtleshell. *What more to say?*
　　Oracles unknown to Gentiles came from Jordan.

　We have our civilization, built on myth –
　　the Hero is a Superman,
　　　translated to a God.
　　Yet this is not the kernel, understand.
　The *Logos* is dark *Song of Songs*... bear with
　me. Primal, buoyant node
of CARITAS, unfold.
　Creation came before its code.
　　Your kelson was its mast – your love its pith.

　　　　　　　　　　　6.6.23

44

She's moving upstream, toward the source.
   With all your schoolcraft, Henry
      packed in the hold.
      Mementos of Menominee
   inexplicable tunes that make you hoarse
 to memorize   peppy phenomena
burgeoning from cold
  cracked cases of ice... *realia*
   outside the magnetism of your compass.

   Your hear the iron heartbeat of a train
      pacing cross-diagonals
         pinioned (over the river).
      The engineer, in overalls
    minds his fire-box under pouring rain.
   This matrix of phenomena
was always here, before
 your quantities of giddy quanta,
   Bohr (Bohm senses blackness whole again).

   Likewise the template of your dome, Latrobe
      veritable task, ineffable
         was flesh and blood already.
      Brain Science Center. Cain and Abel
    out of the cradle of her womb... *O Globe*
 all out of joint! One copper mite?
'*Tis enough, Milady.*
   This root of man's greed – will set it right...
      Venus Beats All, the pencil said. So let it probe.

6.10.23

II

45

At the turbid axle of the Mississippi
  at St. Louis, where the Arch
    plants its soaring prong
    like praying mantis on the march –
  steel shining in the sun like Mercury
  – right there, across the river
looms a salience as strong
  as forking speech (Cahokia).
    Mute lips, out of tumultuous clay.

A tumulus. Amid a flurry of fictions.
  Minds dream and speculate
    mouths fabricate
    and Paradise we illustrate
  around a stone casket. Interdictions
of the gods, the falls of Icarus
are ours – always too late.
  Tell how, wrath-wraith, *e pluribus
    unum*? How chant Whitman-*eleisons*?

Love is strong as death, murmurs the song
  of Solomon, the song of songs.
    We do not reckon how.
    The shadow of a tree prolongs
  life into evening… and beyond. The gong
resounds; with azure splash, the dolphin
arcs flamboyant Now;
  the arms of your Beloved One
    enfold – *Charis* beyond all strife, all wrong.

6.11.23

46

Perverted fabrication of untruth
  is craven service to power
    yet also an unwitting
  nod (like tall grass to the mower)
unto simple veracity – its razor scythe.
 In florid swamps, marred long ago
the wasted king is boxing
 all his secrets... *These will grow*
 new horns, to blow across my voting booth.

 Yet still the Secret rests. Deeper in mind
    than Ariel's plummet (*full fathom*
     five). A mindful thing.
    Of brain matter, its rivery hum.
   *Matière de Bretagne (*Maryam will find
  in Magdala, mayhap). Zoroaster's
molten Magi-ring...
Saturnian carousel of Easter's
  lookout (round whose sepulcher she pined).

 The Jordan flows through swamps like this, toward
    the Dead Sea. Toward the salt-
     engulfing Mississippi.
    Out of her glittering Ocean vault
   Night bears the Milky Way (great many-splendored
  galaxy). Out of your riverine birth-canal
a slime-caked soft baby
 is born... in every sleepy *ville*
  a child of the Most High (translate : *adored*).

6.12.23

47

The poet is a ravenous hunter
  in wastelands of Arabia.
    Poets shouldn't vote
  he said (the Knoxville runaway).
  The architecture of the scent is here.
 They work together, pray for prey –
the trap works. Note
  the carving of brain-stem corral, *hey*
    ey yo... looks like a kite (or huffy vulture).

  The feathered shadow of a human thought
    speeds by like cheetah camouflage.
      Trompe-l'oeil, sharpened
    in its sheath of persiflage.
   These pagans are not holy men – they rot
  like any carrion, yodel
the ranks of dungeoned
  theologians (idle
    in hell). It was some Hellenistic plot.

  Scanning prehistoric blueprints, Benjamin
    I thought of you. Conceptual dome
      or Shakespeare's happy cap,
    your marble shines in its turtle-kingdom
  like ivory, or milky cream... republican
 kite-manuscript. Through *Devil's Gap*
on Elsie's mousetrap
  goeth Abraham. He took the rap,
    the last full drinking-cup – to rise again,
  transhuman.

6.14.23 (Flag Day)

48

The scribes and scholars of experience
   thirsting for a logical facsimile
      miss the touchstone.
   Each vernacular, last family
is imbued with rough, unfiltered evidence –
charisma of one local saint
who (in an undertone)
   will make the sufferer's complaint
      her own (night zephyr of benevolence).

This all goes back to dry, salt Palestine.
   The rabbi was a tall *Nazir*
      who chanted, smiled
      and witnessed, far and near
   to his spellbinding *Shekinah*-vision –
his mantle of *charisma*-hope.
Plain truth was wild
   as a gazelle, sweet as Merope...
      deep desert prey for primitive Orion.

He passed it on. *Here, take this cup.*
   You will go into neighborhoods
      of hoods and warlords,
      fearful wolf-infested woods
   of misery... and you will lift them up.
   Pray to the spirit of the Dove –
she solders swords
   to brimming, broken bowls of love.
      Her power is COSMOS; her steel's a hoop.

6.14.23

49

The loneliness of the long-distance… person.
　The knowledge your parents are gone.
　　And grandparents.
　　And all your neighbors, who remain
　with all their foibles and their febrile passion
must also take that way, alone –
last fearsome descent.
Jesus wept with the mourning ones
　gathered by the grave of Lazarus. Amen.

Melville's melancholy would not lift.
　He too *sang in his chains like the sea*
　　for *la condition humaine.*
　　Snarled with wounded, offended pity
　for the confidence-men – their demonic grift
turning the great river's meanders
to a smoke of phantom gain.
　How the busy frauds and panders
　　squander limpid hours… life's pure gift

and smudge the shy, uncanny morning light
　of childhood grace and innocence
　　with malice (vain delusion).
　　The wide river glints in silence;
　conveys the constellations in its flight.
　Anguish in solitude, at night
swirls with salt fusion
　into that Gulf of human fright.
　　Only the moon remains (sweet affectionate might).

6.15.23

50

55 years ago this spring, the milky-
　honey prism-king was murdered
　　suddenly – in Memphis,
　　near Big Muddy river-rood.
　Next door, on Cecil St., my neighbor Ruby
as a child, playing on the street
(hardscrabble neighborhood
　in old Montgomery) met that sweet
　　young Reverend… walking to his ministry.

She told me this across the fence, the other day.

　Today is *Bloomsday* – and Henry Flower's
　　flown into his octagon gazebo
　　　at subtle 310 Cecil St.
　　Et in Arcadia Ego
　and glides around the grotto of the Mower.
　That dusty fellow there – garbage
collector, heavin'-ho?
　Your *matière de Bretagne* mirage,
　　with artful *maudit* maid… his shadower?

I have been to the mountaintop, we heard him say.

　There are signs everywhere. Roadsigns,
　　outsized inn signs. In farmland
　　　of Franconia (a Gaulish
　　　realm betwixt St. Croix and Scandia,
　　in Minnesota) a tall *trompe-l'oeil* island –
a *fabricated steel, polycarbonate and neon*

replica of the LORRAINE MOTEL.
  Here's the Park pkg. lot... where's the garden?
  May be a vision only *J-Joan* understands.

The moral arc of history... bends toward N'Orleans.

  At midway, in St. Louis, one steely arc
    lifts upwards, like a sigh
      of aspiration. *Come Jubilee*
    we'll all be free. Someday.
    These 50 states of disunion left their mark.
   Green with envy, an absinthe wormwood
Ray tested mortality
  for MLK... only a stand-in for avoided
    LOVE was he. Only an absence in the dark.

The maid of Lorraine cleaned up his disarray.

  My tale's a patchwork palimpsest – no mystery.
    We are one family, claimed King.
      Out of the heart-springs
      of the motherland, pours understanding –
    that *a sword shall pierce your own heart*, Mary.
   Magdalen gathered up the rags,
swept the dusty wings
  in the sepulcher. Rolled up the flags.
    That unknown soldier in the yard... he's calling me.

Come walk with me, green sprout – down Lilac Way.

6.16.23

51

to my father

This rough-looking unsmiling man, in the black-
   white photo, wearing thick glasses.
    Cigarette in thin lips.
   A string of heavy just-caught bass
  dangling from his hand – ready to haul back
 to camp. He's caught unawares
(on such fishing trips
  he brings no camera). And he scares
   me, a little. He's my father... on his own hook.

Amid the submergency of sea-going Holy Books
   the book of *Jonah* is an outlier.
    A riddling zen koan.
   The querulous prophet's out of humor
  after all his trials in the whale's dark nooks.
 Like a figure in a laughing-glass
that anxious, righteous man
 is reproved on high. *Nineveh's ok, you ass.*
  Find peace at home – put down your jukes.

Only a spectral photograph remains
   of my lapsed fisherman, swallowed up
    by Magellanic clouds
   of time. *Clean the inside of the cup,*
  proclaims that prophet of deep lilac lanes.
 We are as blind as quantum bees
humming through shrouds
 of Noah's ark... Hart's reveries.
  En route to incandescent Gulf, on fish we'll sup.
              6.18.23 (Father's Day

52

A new-minted penny flashes its bright disk
   through translucent ripples, right
      at Ocean River's source
      (somewhere north of Itasca).
   The stream moves; the coin, dawn to dusk,
is still. So a brook flows under the chapel
that holds my parents' ashes.
   Not Lethe, but Minnehaha... not in Hell
      but where *all shall be well.* Only ask

and it shall be opened for you : realm of wingèd Jonah.

   The steel alloy that lifts the Gateway Arch
      is a fusion of materials...
         a confluence of thought
      and measurement, that reconciles
   Many and *One.* Emancipation on the march
blossoms in mutual trust – *Liberty*
of, by, for the people. What
   my dear dark Penny in the Texas tree
      willed by those willows... *Jubilee.* Watch!

6.19.23

53

In this country (ignore the neoclassical frieze
  and statuary) heroes are not translated
    to Mt. Olympus. That
  is maintained for thespian celebrity
  (immortal movie stars). Life is a breeze
for them, and thus for us – Time
pulls a rabbit out of its hat.
  Gravity grows light; we're on our knees.
  Parsley, sage, rosemary and thyme.

  These days the radio blares only news.
    It's hard to take. Someone
      is hurt again... someone
      didn't make it. John Donne?
    No Man Is Still An Island (Newport Blues
  Festival – Bob Dylan).
Jazz Festival, son.
  Our folk travail such far horizon.
    See yon scrawny hobo-ghost? Your mother, hon.

  Who then is our hero, America? We know.
    With merciful eye upon her crazy
      husband, globular
      Latrobe... sketching Persephone
  in Hades, for the dome (south to N.O.).
  A limping metaleptic strophe
facing her son... downriver.
  Last *J*-stroke (*closing-time*). So loaf!
  For the Son of Man *comes as a slave, Hobo.*

6.22.23

54

The sun diminishes from St.John's Day
  and bonfires on the hills of Eire
    are elegiac (*aye*).
  What smolders in the poet's heart
  will not burn out, not fade away –
the flame of everlastingness
refines the trivia
  of everyday. To the fire we pray.

  I was pondering that Finnish smithy, where
    the architects of forgery
      framed simulacra
    of the river's molten, surging plea...
    your seething heart, *ancien grand-père.*
  That mongrel, Creole, metaleptic-
epileptic *Sun-Ra*
  plants her Mardi Gras climacteric
    right here – a N'Orleans arc, Lorraine *affaire.*

  The spooky G that haunted Richard III
    the dead man in the marble crypt
      the Masonic pyramid
    flickering through charred manuscript
    – these are but signage... representing *me.*
  In the *Masonic Brain Center*
across the street, the lid
  cracks open – Life, from sepulcher
    comes back. Bees hymn their summer threnody.

6.23.23

55

That this panoply of one mild summer day
  might be the figment of a dream –
   the ballast of illusion.
   That force-field of a stream
 is *change* (carries everything away)
 – yet, though the soul, often, gets lost
somehow the heart stays one –
tonic the music misses most.
  Black Elk hewed memory (*ey hey*).

We circle and encircle *Same* and *Other*
  to protect an infant innocence
   we had forgot, somehow.
   Troy shudders with experience.
  Ophelia is dead – Cain is your brother.
 I have watched the Minotaur
from afar... *Get thee below.*
 *His crude goat-smell is more
  than poetry corrals – his name is* WAR.

Light breeze of summer evening; peacefulness.
  Rain came today. It was
   like light, immaculate
  (pure, simple, innocent). Psyche's
 the climax of the gods (their gentleness,
 their grace). *Potamus* (river-god)
can hardly wait
 to meet her, once again... O Lord
  your delta thunders up ahead (*Atlantis*).

6.25.23

56

The Mississippi journeys home to the sea.
  The river's always on its way.
    So what we know of time
    weaves and meanders, ceaselessly;
  a serpent Möbius, knotting reality
with unspent rings. Her labyrinth
conceals an unsolved crime.
  Primordial wormwood, absinthe
    green... its poison ricocheting back to me.

Every hero is a prodigy – a prodigal child.
  She climbs from folktale orphanage
    to face the deep monster
    lurking in our sleep. A personage
  like Joan of Arc, both steely and mild;
after her blood-curdling trial
even the beast loves her.
He is humanity disfigured, after all –
  Minotaur in the heartland (home, defiled).

And the beast is a fraud, like slippery Geryon –
  popular idol, brutal mirage.
    In the wasteland of his dustbowl
    children forget the shady camouflage
  of benevolent trees... the stream rippling on
beneath somnolent summer leaves.
Mississippi, roll.
This equilibrium our cosmos weaves
  is made of light, is grace. *Let UNION be our unison.*

6.26.23

57

Clear the air, make straight the roads!
  Plant lanthanum in the asphalt!
    These river-curves
  outline your sketchy sky-vault
like Latrobe (detailing his antipodes).
His dome's a small Ionian marble,
made of brain-swerves –
 his capitol's a *Tempest*-bauble,
  tipsy Cap (colossal cup from Rhodes).

Rays of flickering uncertainty
  wave over his brow – like a quantum
    strobe, or maybe Moby-
  Dick. Reality's thought-streams,
like whooping cranes over Missouri,
plunge by that Gateway Arch's
immobility
 – and the current, curling, smoothly lurches
  to a still whorl. *Look below, Henry.*

On the muddy floor of the bottomland, I see
  one copper penny from Venus,
    glimmering in its light
    (so seemingly remote from us).
  Its craggy face, its wistful harmony
remind me of grey-hearted *Jonah*
warbling through the night
 (mourning). Graceful *Sophia*,
  yodeling through the human dome. *O Sea...*

6.28.23

58

The fireworks are already booming in the dark
  five nights before the 4th.
    Just a masquerade
  in memory of one painful birth
of partial freedom (*History's a lark!*).
Down the road, the Stone Arch Bridge
curves its enfilade
  (first – ever) from limestone ledge
    to ledge, across the river... *Twin, mark.*

  Twins were sacred monsters – Tom could tell.
    The mirror's vertigo slips by
      your mental guardrail.
    Poetry? Poe? (Give them a try.)
  The *Rio* murmurs... *Ferry to/from Hell.*
John's sleeping on the bank.
He's sung his last wassail.
  Ate locusts, honey – sniffed at rank.
    The generals will listen. *Treat them well –*

y'all are children of the Most High God.
  A shadow looms across the stream.
    Wingèd, like dove
  or insect... curved like a turtle-dome
or *kingdom come.* Don't ask me to explain, Brod.
The crow flies to the Delta – returns
to the ark (for love).
  YHWH makes men from stones... urns
    open. Jordan's lifting leaf from sod.

6.29.23

59

The *Son of God*, and *Man* – an unknown soldier.
   We have the Hellenistic fictions,
      Galilean tracks…
   but the tall Rabbi's depictions
   slant away – like tree-shades from some August memoir.
   Where is that copper coin of the realm
which correlates our acts
   with a central Good? Who grips the helm?
   I only know : *where Love is, there You are.*

If I could paint a cosmic panorama
   it would be a rolling scroll, slow-moving,
      like John J. Egan's
      Grandeur of the Mississippi. Sing,
   Walt Whitman! There's your pivotal drama,
   beneath the lilacs' purple shade…
your humble veterans –
   companions in his last parade.
   The scroll whorls at St. Louis… (one clay ring).

And I recall that temple of *Equality*
   Latrobe contrived, in Washington –
      a dome like Shakespeare's *cap*
      of happiness… green oak-leaf crown
   or Golgotha of *Brain Science.* Your little tree,
   Jesse… hidden in a library.
Whatever will mayhap
   in May, or in July… your love *shall be.*
   Love turns the stars (invisibly, indivisibly).

7.1.23

60

Rhode Islander R. Williams was a prophet.
  A spiritual enthusiast.
    And yet he apprenticed
    to Sir Edward Coke... that vast,
   worldly gymnast of the City – of *quodlibet*
  please the people (*and your Majesty*
of course). He said :
 Reason is the life of the law. Nay,
   the common law itself is nothing else, but

   reason (*that law which is perfection*
   of reason). Thus... *Eternal Life*
    is optional. We're
    gifted with your gilded knife
   of preternatural communion
   – we *animale compagnevole*
(per Dante Alighieri
  and the Stagirite). *O Sophie*
   of Byzantium... Jerusalem... look down!

   For we – *conceived in liberty, and*
    dedicated to the proposition –
     come to that crossroad
    Hamlet faced. *Give me that man*
   who is not passion's slave... this rotten land!
  The canoe (like a *mandorla*) stays
in midstream; its copper load
   bears down on Abraham... weighs
     heavily. *Lift sail, American!* (Understand.)

                                                7.2.23

61

A young turtle plops from a log into the stream
  like a gray-green stone, like an unknown soldier.
  Concentric ripple-rings with seamless silence
 glide, expand... melt into the flow.
The turtle's only an emerald shadow, now –
a trick of sunlight? Maybe a shade
 of *Joan*, of *Jonah*... *Juliet*? The shade is dense.

  Euclid measured his *radii*, his sunny science,
   Mediterranean. The mind discovers
  these logical curves, conjunctions...
 a kind of marriage of convenience
so absolute, it shines with joy...
almost a real wedding (at Cana, or Cahokia).
 That world's a lovely *mandorla* – a top, a toy.

  This pain in my heart is more convincing, though.
   More final (steady beat, incessant).
  Something has to give, when the well goes dry
 and the stream is air, and the bowl broken...
someone has to die. We have been here before.
The grey bird lifts her wings;
 a turtledove calls, from her everlasting spring

  and, as it turns out, our philosophical conjectures
   are only folded into a poem. The turtle
  is a submarine – the river is a stream
 of consciousness – the *Son of Man*,
the *Mother of Man*, is *Everyone* (unknown
soldier). The young scribes swim to Philadelphia.
 Lives, fortunes, honor... River's lambent auspices.

                     7.4.23

62

Something moving there, something bigger than us.
   Blind people see it better than we.
    They sense it. Relentless,
    silent, constant... ignoring you
   as it flows toward its fate (azure *quietus*).
  Hart Crane, his *milk of paradise*
poured from Atlantis
  met that Gulf himself (caverns of ice) –
   nouveau New World, *Christophe Coulombe* (Ouroboros).

  Now we see both ways (microscopes, telescopes)
   darkly. Each genius of the hearth
    holds close the family
   while gazing far (toward Earth
  or *Ursus Major*). Who can grasp these ropes?
 Your heart's invisible Red River
keeps the mustang free –
  run, stallion! Speed, classy whisperer!
  Pindaric feet thunder with human hopes.

  Earthworks of ancient clay (immemorial
   mudpies) twirl off, like eddies
    from the Mississippi.
   All is water, muttered Thales
  (old Ionian philosopher, conjectural).
  Yet I can see his point. *La mer
est notre Baptistère* –
  we search for some communion
   there. Slave Moses is *l'enfant royal.*

                        7.5.23

63

i.m. *Elijah P. Lovejoy*

Every hamlet has its Hamlet, so it seems.
　Each Denmark has its lion's den –
　　Mark, *Twain*. The stream
　　is more than you imagined, Hen.
　That *Connecticut Yankee* spends his dreams
　on *Camelot*, on *Joan of Arc*...
Huck, off the beam
　and swimming (for his Noman's ark).
　Hopeful scribblers transcribe their screams...

　like F. Scott, in St. Paul. "Jay Gatsby
　　was a con man, with a heart – unlike
　　　Manco Capac." Read
　　my late critique, thrown in the lake
　　of fire : *Humankind can't bear too much reality*
　(mimed the professor). St. Louis
drove Lovejoy, indeed
　over to Illinois... *He's in Alton, boys.*
　　Let's go. Free speech means poverty.

　These halcyon days, Horatio... are leaning short.
　　Like that murmuring wall in Alton
　　　I would make a monument
　　　lifted above the scrim of passion,
　　Walt. With wingèd *Victory*, athwart
　a marble mainmast – tried by wind.
Angel of sweet descent!
　Rapt, yourself, with painful mind
　　of human woe... she croons, *Take heart.*

7.6.23

64

The background music is often overlooked,
  unsourced – subliminal ambience,
    folding back upon
    itself. Time's transience
  (in someone's heart) is raw, not cooked.
 The whole of history's an elegy
wild Mary Magdalen
 composed for us – from tragedy
    (her hollow shock). It's all been booked.

I see John Egan's river-panorama,
  suffused in bright Edenic green –
    with prehistoric mounds,
    earth-circles, Easter Island
  stone idols... a kind of mandala
 for *New World* – spirit-map
Black Elk propounds.
 Portable heaven-vault. Sky-lap.
  Our planetary Turtledove's regalia.

The stream skims on, a constant undertone;
  my hymns are but a fumbled plummet-
    stone. The scroll, stretched
    open... frames a small casket.
  It was the Grail of our imagination
 (every traveler's communion).
A jade crypt, etched
 across six sides. The Magdalen
  concealed it, in Jerusalem... (unknown).

7.7.23

65

This brown serpent is an oscillation of waves.
  Sturdy, constant, flickering.
    A stream of particles,
    immeasurably thickening
  and gaining mass (toward the Bayou). Braves
 were gathered here, 10,000 years
ago… a quickening
 preceding Susan Quick (Jessie Ophelia's
  grand-mère). Here lie Mississippian graves.

 Who are we? Maybe our stately paddle-wheeler
   hosts a Copenhagen tragedy –
     Elsinore (Frayn's quantum
   comedy). Or *Certainly Uncertainty*
 (by Born, Bohr & de Broglie). *Send a feeler,*
 worm. This dust was… Richard III.
Light's on a spectrum
 between red and blue – like human nature.
   Truth is fact… and what we make of it, my dear.

 This American river washes a turtle's back.
   That's the story, that's the myth.
     A curve, a painted rainbow…
   would it were so. Ophelia was blithe
 and Hamlet loved her, then… all went to wrack
 (alas). America's a broken family
(*Everything Must Go*).
 Still… azure snakeskin shines, along that lee.
   Word is, the Turtledove is monitoring Merrimack.

7.9.23

66

Troubled by our fractioned commonweal,
   I traveled to the river-spring –
      Itasca. *Veritas*
      Caput. Ozaawindib was guiding
   Schoolcraft, then; unveiled the source, the real
   headwaters of her Nile. Like *Ymir*,
the *First Man*, she was;
   a trans-twinslator – your own *Enaree*,
      Henry. *Longfellow, Scythian* (with sex appeal).

July be ripely muggy, here in the Twin Cities;
   it's almost tropical now (outside
      the *Brain Science Center*).
      The warring colors (blue and red –
   York, Lancaster) wounded Ophelia would appease
   with violet. With rue (by Lake Plantagenet,
mayhap). Under the armor
   of yon sturdy swaybacked pine, an ingrate
      baby cedar creeps aloft... (his crown to seize).

At the park entrance, near the Headwaters,
   a small gray sculpture (like a fountain
      ornament). The curving
      locks, the loving arms of *Dove-Woman*
   release an infant turtle-flock she harbors,
   toward the surging river (just ahead).
Our mother, molding
   river-clay... to cups, to bowls. Love led
      Latrobe, also. Wisdom's an ark (for neighbors).

7.14.23

67

On the Ides of July, all is wave, not particle.
  Heat rays off white buildings escape
    through transparency windows.
    The planet is a ripened grape
  in a burning smokehouse (read the article?).
O monotonous determined flow
of Time... *so it goes.*
  The riverbend, in its undertow
    aspires to maelstrom – circles, umbilical.

Latrobe, the architect and boatbuilder
  set off for New Orleans, following
    his eldest son (fever
    took him too). Your sense of spiraling
  dynamic symmetry... *that London dome-welder's*
a sunflower. Ionian marble
gleams like flesh, forever;
  the Capitol – a geometrical marvel –
    only a parable for equity (legal... tender).

I'm shaping a whirlpool, or black hole
  forged in Kythira, out of copper.
    Love burns like fire
  that cannot be assuaged, my dear.
  My plummet is a penny – bears the whole
  Shakespearean phantasmagoria,
the river's muddy mire.
  Profile of Abraham (*trompe-l'oeil* realia).
    Heals rot in Elsinore. Twain's ark (Joan's role).

7.15.23

68

In that rippling-clear Itasca brook, I found
    a little keepsake stone. Triangular,
      mud-brown. Faint greens
    and yellows... plain. An unknown soldier.
    Stone stays steadfast in the stream. Ground
    camouflaged as earthy water,
the way a grassblade leans
    its polished copper sword to summer wind.

    The Mississippi starts remembering the sea
      at infancy. Moses, in his Nile-
        cradle, grows stony too –
      ready to remake, in his own style,
      the Pharaoh's Isis-ritual. And *what will be
will be*, mutters determined Hamlet –
*I will remember thee,
    Ophelia.* Meanwhile, on Galilean Street
    that unknown rabbi flips Rome's panoply.

    Fear, like a boat unmoored upon the water
      is a constant companion – sadness
      and dread in its wake.
      Still, the river remembers the *Yes*
    of *Ocean* – ring where time becomes a sphere;
    and I follow Latrobe, the architect,
on the arc of his Ark
    to New Orleans... where sea-birds project
      high phosphorous G-chords. Let Atlantis appear.

*

Dust of foreboding settles on the capital.
Money twists the knife of grievances.
The Confidence-man (that *Angry Man*) dances
to his own contorted tune... stirs the unreal.

The war is a froth of petty instances.
Building estrangement, summoning bad will.
What happened to good neighborhood? The well
is the same, for red and blue... (*Ahura Mazdā* says).

The midnight pool of human loneliness is deep
as the sea. O *Consciousness*, wake from your sleep!

I dreamt of an infinite benevolence.
A lovingkindness we have yet to feel.
Our *imago* of Good is but a turtleshell...
yet we perceive the curve's green radius.

Cracks in the facade, grease down the wall...
the fair *Republic*? Some forsaken toy, useless.
The kids have eaten sour grapes; and wilderness
creeps back, across the marble outline of the Mall.

*

As each thing of beauty is a final end
  good in itself, pleasing to all
    so is that child perfect,
  skipping toward her very playful
Source (whose loving ways will never bend).
So the architect's articulate *Logos*

will make the stones reflect
  one interstitial *Word*, uniting us –
  brave Lincoln logarithm. Dove, descend!

  Love and Law, Walt Whitman crooned.
    The common good, which undergirds
      the whole spectrum of joy –
    the rainbow's promise, lifting shards
  of hope into shared happiness. The wound
 to heal; the orphan and the veteran
to sense life's poetry.
  From deep in far-off time's grain bin
    to lift redemption's almond (long-marooned).

  So the intractable pebble, that makes no sound
    the unknown soldier, who resists the flow
      seems to float like pumice now
    toward the Gulf. Like that Frisbee fellow
  in his acorn coracle – lightweight, round –
  adrift down muddy Arthur Street
in Hopkins, long ago;
  in your mother's tale, not yet complete.
    She's warbling an endless summer sound.

                                    7.18.23

69

A lonesome cardinal, lapped in evening cedars
  blares his scarlet clarion
    driving each chiseled cry
    like a nail into the day's coffin.
  The river, bending near, listens... hears,
  somehow. So the blind physicist
entranced, will spy
  the curve of her equation – will persist
    until a radius lays out the surface of its spheres.

That cardinal's number is importunate
  (an operatic caterwaul).
    Love is strong as death,
    she wails... *the readiness is all.*
  Her redness is no shame. Love is a trait
  no traitor understands – his taste
is lost (rancid as wrath).
  Fly to me, Beloved! Make haste!
  Thy song's my key (transposable, innate).

The sweet curves of your peregrine river
  whorl in a *J*-spring, child.
    Where cedars stand...
    where unrequited love goes wild.
  For love is the heartwood of *Logos*, forever –
  our Lincoln *logos*, just and true.
So close... it's in your hand.
  So near... it's midmost (me and you).
    There is no wrath, in Turtledove's *Circumnavire.*

7.20.23

70

Here, in this rickety 8-fold gazebo
which is my body, two rivers flow –
one red, one blue. They quarreled long ago.
I'd raise a violet pavilion, to be their shadow.

South of Cairo ran a single river road.
Rhodos, it was – built by good William.
It marked a limit for *imperium* –
a radiant circumference (one human fold).

The cosmos plants in every human soul
GOOD, for all seekers – simple, intellectual...

Stand up then, Human! Cast off your chains
of servile bigotry – spite, enmity!
Sniff out that limpid sense of liberty –
a morning air, conducting joy's refrains!

In far-off Chartres (Louisiana?) once
a Pythagorean monk named Thierry
taught how from *Union*, came *Equality* –
upon *l'arc-en-ciel* of LOVE (*la vraie plaisance*).

7.22.23

71

Those seamless interlocking Inca boulders
  on the summit of Cuzco, mirror
    ethereal wave-forms
  at *Fonte Gaia* (in the *centro*
of republican Siena). Nature's alders
 mold our wooden clogs. They are
our mothers, fathers. *Worms*
 are we, Horatio – Ophelia's there.
  The capstone's US (anonymous soldiers).

  The center of space is the center of time, Imogen
  imago. This grainy continuum
    is only human construct
    (something like an American poem,
  Poe). The water here is clear as frozen
air. Here the turtle shapes her Dominican
Republic; now the mocked
 Word, that transatlantic woman
  plants her sooth (north south east west)... *anon.*

  So the waves glissando to crescendo, Verdi –
   a modulation anonymity cannot
    gainsay (mute, speechless
    as she is). They gather to a knot,
   these heartwaves, bloodwaves – where the Missouri
  meets the Mississippi. *Down like a Pawnee...*
Like a game of bloody chess
 at the apex of American glory
  an assassin strikes the hero-saint (slow-painted memory).

7.23.23

72

Ruby, my friendly next-door neighbor
  near the Brain Science Center
    grew up in Montgomery,
  Alabama – as a child she'd encounter
  Martin Luther King, the young pastor
walking to his office. There's a river
flows from you, from me,
  from everybody... justice its measure.
  And red is that rose of River *R*.

Thus out of Memphis rose the fiery ghost
  of a milky king, beyond all kings;
    phantom of a smiling child
  who flickers by on moth wings
  in your sleep... lifting a broken host.
  Half a loaf, so you might share
and make it whole. Mild
  ceremony, fair and square –
  a wedding, celebrated coast to coast.

The youngsters are playing a summer game
  out in the grass, at the Brain
    Science Center – each
    tosses a ball... And I recall again
  that *Game of Spheres*, of Cusa's fashioning.
  A parable of chance and accident
and hopeful will – to reach
  that matrix of benevolent intent
    (ineffable wellspring we cannot name).

Indeterminacy, at the microcosmic minimum
of quantum reality, oscillates in waves
through the mobs of opinion, the braves
of avarice optimization (their power-hum).

Geryon was his name, for the Florentine –
serpentine monster of fraud, deceit.
Confidence-Man, for Melville – a neat
card trick, to sell downstream (*Has-Bean*).

We must turn back to peace, from enmity
a violet whispers... a moss-green penny.

Through a narrow clay channel she proceeds.
Her name is *Rio del Espiritu Santo.*
Like the bumped ball in the game, she'll go
wobbling toward the Gulf... where azure bleeds

into ocean sky – vast, open, booming.
Keeping time (like your heart's core,
Hamlet). *Atlantis...* and something more –
tomorrow's Gateway (human Arc, looming).

America was not a tribe, but an idea;
    yet ideas grow from memory.
      For the blind physicists
    inching along an arcane pathway
   reality itself is an idea... (*adagia*
  of island-crossings, shade). See
next door, brain scientists –
   the holy Thou inflects each human Me.

THE GREEN RADIUS

Green gyroscope hovers... *hallelujah.*

A turtle has 4 symmetrical, clawed legs
   and a painted shell (like a mandala
      or dome). She is a home
      away from home, or *at* home – *Roma*
   traveler through Eire, on Lincoln logs –
or America. Grows by itself
(her shell) it seems. A kingdom
   like a panorama... scrolled on shelf
      wherever freedom swims – life breeds, begs.

The timbre of her travelogue, Horatio
   was murmured by Ophelia
      tuned to the stream.
      Her vocals (*che sera, sera*)
   hurtle down... her wispy oratorio
only a willow, bent in grief.
Love – unconsoled. Supreme.
   Dawn rises, light beyond belief.
      It is Ophelia, mourning... Easter, so.

7.24.23

73

A lone cricket's monotone *scree*
  like a child's arpeggios
   along a plastic comb.
  I am beneath my cedar gazebo's
octagon – waning summer's part of me.
 An architecture built of ruin
dreams of a happy home.
 Where is the way to it, again?
  Downriver, New Orleans. Green cypress tree.

 Fetid lagoons cannot decay the wood
  of cypress window-frames. Blue lacquer,
   red… *those extra coats*
  will cost you, friend. Problems occur
  when gamesmanship scratches the common good.
 Your rivalry's a quicksand guile
(deep fakes, bought votes);
 yon high bell in the Campanile
  unhorses every strutting neighborhood.

 The curve of a simple boat mimics the wave,
  echoes the surf. Sand-castles
   soften, melt away
  where the horizon line wrestles
  the shore. One azure arc frames the grave
 across the river, mirrors the sea-
light of earliest day.
 Time boomerangs through memory.
  Union, Equality… (redemption's architrave).

7.30.23

74

August, the month of Roman bronze.
  Helmet, breastplate, shield…
    to be at home in iron.
    Not so the delicate field
  cricket – chanting melancholy tones
 out of a lightweight ebony
casket (her own).
  A Stradivarius with legs (tiny)
    whose aria's an elegy (*vox clamans*).

  My mother's painting from the late '60s –
    a landscape, with grain elevator
      and brown boxcars.
    Framed by elm trees (almost bare).
   The scene's a symphony in hulking grays.
  Her father built it. His blueprints
like stone larvae in jars
  lift these seed-revival tents,
    Madonna del Parto… your labor-sepulchers.

  These emblems of my time and memory
    ripple down the riverbend.
      Light (unaccountable
    breeze) leads them on, friend.
  Sophia might have been a Quaker bee-
  hive, in some Willa Cather tale –
or your own farm table,
  Grandma. Turtle's a type of whale.
    Isis-canoe – a kind of Easter mystery.

                                    8.1.23

75

In the poem, *Frisbee*, the hero, sails
  down Arthur St. (in a folded-
    paper tugboat-hat).
  This bedtime *Argonautica* (molded
by my mother) lingers in mind... prevails,
somehow. Like Miss Padgett – *Padgy* –
poinsettia-scarlet
 in her Christmas dress. She nicknamed me
  *Jackson (*like that populist Hercules).

But that reminds me of another Jackson –
  Jackson Quick, the Mississippi
    river-pilot. Died
  aboard a hospital ship, in 1863
  outside Vicksburg (serving the Union).
 Jessie Ophelia's father, he was...
full-fathom-fived.
 Truth's a taut bow, per Heraclitus;
  only a canoe can make crosscurrents one.

Plutarch underwrote Shakespeare, I guess
  along with subtlest Michel.
    Osiris, in his cricket-
  casket, croons... *all shall be well.*
  Remember Osip, and François – Paris,
 their cricket-city – artisans
of splendor's parapet;
 rejoin the cosmic *citoyens*
  in New Orleans... your motherland, Isis.

8.2.23

76

This was the day of Jack. *This was the day*
    that Jack *put the* Angry Man *in a box.*
      That furious Bedlamite
      had stolen the keys and broken the locks
    and Jack was determined to make him play
  fair. And my granddad (*Ravlin, Jack*)
built his house one night
  on the River Road – out of solid brick.
    My mother was born there (in 1928).

  Padgy, the scarlet schoolteacher, called me
    Jackson, in honor of Granddad
      and me. She was loving
      and kind. When Jack Kennedy died
    I was mortal sad – we shared a birthday
  at the end of May (Pentecost,
it was – day of the diving
  Dove). When the world seems lost
    it is, little boy. It is lost, really –

  almost for good; and you will grow to know
    more than you want to know (like
      Jack). *Stand up for the country,*
      then, and be a man, little tyke!
    This river, flowing through, so slow
  is full of ghosts... is history,
burnt at the stake.
  The River J (for *Jeanne, Jackie*
    and *Jack*) is clear, is changeful. *Muddy*... wash me so.

                                          8.3.23

77

Last week two from the Bakken Trio played
  at Dick and Anna's – by the River Road,
    upon ancient instruments
    (cello, violoncello, *circa* 1600).
  Concord of *sostenuto* cricket-hymns, they made.
 Beauty and goodness harmonize
and violence relents
 for once... scales tremble (sympathize).
  To summer's dark the cricket fleet will fade.

Bellerophon rode *Pegasus* toward
  Chimera (frothing "7-7"
    versus Judgement Day) –
  a test of fraud opposing heaven.
  Bitter truth will be his last reward.
 So murmured *Enaree Tiresias,*
Dove-Woman... Mrs. Sippay.
  Where *cylix* whorls to chelys-chalice
  Raven's cupola-goblet is poured.

Pegasus (the Sea Scout vessel) floats
  the nine musing pioneers
    toward St. Louis –
  where the architect's own arc appears;
  it is a tortoiseshell (that plays nine notes).
 Liz Friedheim raised it from the Gulf
quick as thought flies
 on courier-pigeon... it was no waif
  but *Rio del Espiritu* (a lamp, my dears).

8.7.23

78

The sag of systems that have worked too well
 for too long, breeding vipers
  out of fetid crevices
  of marshland. The *Amnesia Wars*
 with all their noisy battle-cries, the smell
of rancid, brazen lies. And over
all these politic devices
 the Heat Dome, like a voluminous lover
  looms... armorial of late Roman hell.

August, once more – summer's on the wane.
 The crickets, like a *Hallelujah* chorus
  cheep a night vortex
  for slightly-fading sun. Susurrus,
 echoing : *I will not drink this cup again*
until I drink with you anew...
with all the architects
 of human happiness (a vow
  to knot the finial of human pain).

There is one spring from which all waves proceed.
 All curves of dome, all bends of stream
  clay lips of every cup
  and every sinuosity of dream.
 Out at the edges... where the colors bleed.
And you lose the thread – and the Arch
where clouds are lifted up
 must hold you like a cradle (birch?)...
  a Milky Way *ecclesia*. Turtledove's high meed.

8.23.23

79

The little rust-brown agate Jamie found
  in a field by the river, behind the church
    flared a spiral conduit,
    slim as a silver Nile cartouche
  on a maroon (Iron Range) background.
 I wanted Jamie's agate – traded
my toy truck for it;
  like *stone fallen from heaven* (jade)
    it was a plumb-bob (*mark twain*... sound).

 We are a flimsy, fallible microcosm
  of the universe, writ Nicholas
     of Cusa (kindly clerk).
    A penny, under the lethal mess
  of floodwater; the hurricane's calm
 eye. A pilot's touch is quick
where whirlpools lurk.
 Steady as she goes, Fidèle... (flick
   of spindrift seals Persephone's kingdom).

 Psyche... thine agate lamp. *Mn... mn...*
   the stuttering prophet remembers.
    Mnemosyne. Isis
   in her tippy-frail canoe. (Embers
  of Memphis milk-trains rumble... hum
  across the bridge.) *Imogen*
will rise again, he says;
  romance of resurrection... is
    supernatural (Akhmatova-imperium).

8.24.23

80

Now summer's drawing to a close. What shall I sing
  for you, wayfaring stranger?
   Long way from home.
  When the land itself grows stranger,
   and no one knows what-all tomorrow may bring
 (if there is a tomorrow). And the river
is a moving mirror. Some
  invasive species (with a full quiver)
   mimics Canadian thistle – seeds that sting.

  The little crickets' cry is feeble, yet
   they touch their high note (key
    of constancy). An agate
   in the mind. Earth-colored, she...
  yet crystalline (a *Psyche* spider-net).
  An alien geometry;
a corn-fed gate
  into your own (Brain Sci) eternity –
   pure spring of charity (Pascal's checkmate).

  I have a dream... that heavy Incan stone
   of Atahualpa. Fell from heaven,
    camouflaged as earth.
   The silver thread, the Apollonian
  galaxy, was VERITAS (Itascan).
  And you too will sing, Jessie-
Ophelia : *Death*
 is for the Turtledove, milky –
  whose life is green forever (soul Union).

8.28.23

81

Banners jostle, flap, and swivel in the wind
  at the State Fair in St. Paul.
    Under a waning August blaze,
   out of the thronging crowd's festival
  crazy-quilt, one cosmopolitan tide
 surges – uniting widespread streams
in her hurdy-gurdy haze
 of polka, poker, beards, ice-cream.
   And Orpheus (detached octahedron) floats in Mind

  as into Hebrus eddies... (sand). While *Pegasus*
    that old, 2-tiered concrete steamboat
     of mournful *Henry Duplex*
    back-pedals her oaten shepherd's goat-
   flute – rewinds the spring of Brain Science
  and rain (obscure, Itascagate)
to one column of ilex :
 one shady-green lemniscate
   hiding a rose quartz in its stone-grey silence.

  Psyche... thy lamp. Steadfast as a mirror
    whorled in eddies. Sweet lighthouse.
     Your sabbath beehive.
    Vortex out of black-hole emptiness
   humbling eagles' violence with *coulombe*-sentience.
  Reminiscences of 1865.
Some milk-train jive
 from Memphis? Rumored still alive,
   in her soul-chariot (Eli's bright horse of yore).

8.29.23

82

to Edwin Honig

August is over. Zydeco anthems
  animate the crepuscule
   and super Blue Moon...
   beneath her sane and adamant rule
 Lethe whorls to Jordan. *Down on it foams*
 the yellow-jacket Missouri. Treason –
not against Calhoun,
  nor Lincoln... not *the People's* reason...
   but against conscience (whence every soul becomes).

Sea Scouts still test themselves (Odyssean)
  in double-canoes (Manx-catamarine)
   against the Mississippi.
   Yet she's afore them, every morning –
 hoists them, vertical, astride Cahokia. Tall pine
  where the unchartered waters lift
an arc, a kingdom (see?)
 – an Inca stone – Peruvian gift.
   Agate of Vallejo; Lincoln Brigade (*no pasarán*).

The pilot – Quick, with plumb-line gyroscope –
  shepherds the dreaming, mewling lambs.
   François, at Notre Dame
   nods to Beatrice, past all scams;
 Eternity, O Eternity! – sustains our hope.
 This old Parisian undercurrent,
green Louisiana home
  skips down to New Orleans... bent
   toward the sea. Wide *Okean* (azure wave-slope).

8.30.23

83

Long-suffering Celan bids the world adieu
　　into the Seine. Like a sign
　　　for the Prodigal Son
　　who could never, *ma mère*, go home again.
　　What does the Heavenly Family mean to you?
　I think that Mark was riven in twain
by the power of Rome (benign
　Caesar!) – so his Gospel makes plain;
　　a *widerruf* for *Son of Man* (dove-light, come true).

　Spain, take this cup from me! cries out César –
　　a condor molted into dove
　　　by his whimpering brother
　　lost behind the stars. *Jove,*
　　lift your vulture off my chest! We are
　all children of the same father;
this masquerade of Shakespeare
　but a holocaust of all that bother...
　　ABBA, *forgive them*; *they know not what*... (selah).

　I think again of Benjamin Latrobe
　　designer of the Capitol,
　　　embarked to New Orleans
　　to find his son (for burial)
　　and die there, too – sketching his little globe
　the while. I see our Family
of Man, all it maintains
　in spite of violence, rank enmity...
　　(Jay-T, down by the river, wraps him in his robe).

8.31.23

84

Turtle is a terse creature, slow-moving
  in the moving river. Paints a still
    mandala, over time –
  saturates her ebony shell
  with ruby, emerald, sapphire... mesmerizing.
  Bone, dyed with a rainbow sheath
like that glittering rime
  of carapace (train station, underneath).
    Steals into hovering light... a needle's grooving

  transubstantiation (earth-green radius).
    Like arches in the Utah desert
      on a quarter-dollar coin
      art lances straight into the heart
    – with mimicry. César Vallejo is an alias
  (almost?) for Abraham Lincoln –
from head unto the groin
  awash with pity and compassion;
    here a heartbeat meets the silence, in stillness.

  Trompe-l'oeil, trompe-l'oeil. Lincoln, after life
    standing in broad day. At pilot-wheel
      of history – like Jackson
      Quick, like *Son of Man*. Seal
  my heart, like *Turtledove* cleaves to her wife –
  at the gateway, where an agate threads
four spirals round a stone
  to celebrate your feast, at last. Clods
    lean together; glad smiles praise the end of strife.

9.2.23

85

1

Your agate was a lamp for me, *Psyche*
  by Mississippi headwaters;
    your *Santa Cáliz*, your cup
  became my tortoiseshell chelys.
  Libation poured out for Eurydice
 by *Orpheus*, *Apollo* and *Raven*;
where all the birds will sup
 and all the arrogance of men
  be quenched. A *last full measure*, verily.

2

Phantoms gather near St. Louis, at the center
  of the stream; the harp of Saarinen
    lifts up to sky.
  That gateway of all human pain
 frames a *trompe-l'oeil* mandorla there –
binding the shepherd to the wolf
in one salt-spectral eye.
 Con-man and saint meet at the Gulf.
  The ark of *Jeanne d'Arc* hovers... (light as prayer).

3

Drought and famine haunt our pummeled Earth.
  Even the *Rio del Espiritu* might fade
    beneath our pride, our greed.
  The *Doppelgänger's* on parade.
 A type of *Antichrist*, for what it's worth –
that Angry Man *Ahura Mazda*
faced; so shepherds bleed.
 Tammuz, wounded violet – *¡vaya!*
  Your adamant *madre* is... your agate's berth.　　9.5.23

86

The parish church of St. Cecilia
　is modeled on a Roman temple.
　　Yet its massive apse
　where once a marble Caesar (ample,
　overbearing) reigned, is hollow, empty...
save for a minuscule gold cross
and simple, time-lapse
　replica of Leonardo's famous
　　feast (Empire displaced by *Ultima Cena*).

　In my agate mandorla of wizened cedar
　　a maze of three streams whorls
　　　into a salty fourth.
　Memoirs of Civil War recoils
　two centuries upon one spine (water
and blood). Jonah, like a turtledove
floats from the whale's mouth –
　and from a shattered brain-alcove
　　the Phoenix of undying life fans into air.

　These enigmatic shadows mold a masque
　　for simple truth. There is a Law
　　　by which all laws are framed –
　　it marks a path your heart foresaw
　from infancy. Down by the Jordan, John will ask
you – simply – to remember. *Love
is Justice*, he proclaimed.
　It is the wellspring from above.
　　To join this *paisan* feast – your blessèd task.

　　　　　　　　　　　　9.9.23

87

I stamp each letter very laboriously,
  through iron teeth... on this obsolete
   typing machine.
   Recalling the *Stamp Act* debate,
  its ominous clang of yang – its clashing clay.
 And how sweet Benjamin Latrobe –
his domical design
 complete – fled our distracted globe
  to seek his son (a cypress reliquary).

In this land, LAW IS KING – the painful
  Rights of Man trump every foe;
   yet it is not so
   easy. *Ben-ya-min*, from long ago
  lifted a tacit almond rod, under the waterfall.
 A winter bloom – the microcosm
of a four-fold river-flow.
 A mini-Mississippi... (comb
  your hair, Jessie Ophelia – your cup is full).

We seek a Law within the law; a whorl
  of mirrors, cornucopia.
   An old seashell
   sounding Siena's *Fonte Gaia* –
  sphere of Nicolas of Cusa (wisdom's pearl).
 César Vallejo and Old Abe
chant *All is Well*
 there, in that agate astrolabe.
  A gyroscope. *O Star*... blind pilot's Pole.

9.12.23

88

These little eddies that the river makes
　along the margins, where they merge
　　so seamlessly
　　into a wider, slower surge...
　huge Sabbath Day the world forsakes.
　My mutterings along the edge
disturb that ecstasy –
　but just slightly; my brittle pledge
　　to you, Silence, won't break those wakes.

The river-pilot understands just how
　topmast and anchor are attuned.
　　Her Black Sea bottomland
　　rotates the galaxy around –
　her tacit plumbline marries Then and Now.
　Her memory (her mother's muse)
restores each heart turned sand
　with sweet spring-water. That's *the news*
　　that stays news : that's the Eye upon the prow.

This dancing impulse at the river's source
　is calling you... so quietly,
　　so soft, so clear.
　　From your concerns you must give way
　a little... paddle back... adjust your course.
　The good life rests immovably
murmurs the seer
　because it is eternal – see?
　Soul never dies. Dance like a horse!

9.14.23

III

89

The dream of Union is the sweetest dream
  that sailors know. Hamlet, imprisoned
   on board ship, turns round
   toward Elsinore – commissioned
  there, where memory holds seat... *redeem*
 the time. Siege Perilous;
Elijah's ground.
  That grail of human happiness,
    heart's cryptic microcosm... cosmic scheme.

  You lose your way, along a jagged line
   of cracked limestone, across
     the Seine – a lightning flash;
    and find a tiny gate of moss,
   an agate's whorl. Four springs' direction.
  You hear the murmuring of water-
voices, waves made flesh...
  the joy of lambent light and matter
    morphed into a smiling clay reunion.

  And what was finished there has just begun.
    You sense a cornucopia
      unfolding in your heart.
    Self-evident *equalità*
  each one's birthright, the stately ship's kelson.
  All rooted in clear streams
that from a rainbow dart –
  one agate mandorla, whose beams
    pilot this buoyancy (benevolent, humane).

9.16.23

90

I carry an agate from Itasca in my pocket
  when I walk to the River (down
    Cecil St., past
  the Brain Science Center). Crown
  me *Henry Duplex*, Lord – of *Pegasus*, Sea Scout.
 My double is that man from Porlock;
river *Alph* has cast
 me into *caverns, measureless...* rock
  chipped from a diamond. An octahedral sunset

  painted with an eagle feather, on a stone.
   Binaries of good and evil –
    mirror images
   of *Ahriman*, his angry will...
  for our idiotic shadows we must each atone.
 Black Elk makes his upright prayer.
These national mirages
 are our just deserts. So share
  my adobe of humble ashes, prince (compassion).

  Today we celebrate our Constitution –
   out of many States (13)
    came one. Our twin's
   a brutal idiot – he's US, I mean;
  yet *Rio del Espiritu Santo* shines in the sun.
 Big Muddy washes mirrors, even.
Wash away our sins,
 Jordan. MLK's our *Son of Man* –
  fireworks of *Ocean River...* honey, hon.

9.17.23

91

The river speaks with many voices – *glossolalia*
   I can't contain. My mandala
      has its dark patches
   (like my heart). From Lake Itasca
   to the Gulf, it shimmers – serpent's replica.
   Suture the wound, then, with a needle
where the Missouri catches
   hold... and loft a Mississippi paddle-
      wheel, Pawnee, for burial. *Selah.*

   Over a simple smoke-hole in Rhode Island
      tender shades hover, then sail southwest.
         These infant memories
      precede the strife of love and lust,
      the heroes' games of agèd seers (gone blind).
   The heart's *ecclesia* of children –
what your soul must seize
   to enter into that *kingdom of heaven.*
      In azure there, mercy and adoration sound

      their unison. It's close to you – close
         as that old man, walking up the path
            ahead of you. Your father,
         or his ghost, Hamlet. The end of wrath
      rings like a cicada from your *chelys*,
   Orpheus – her tortoiseshell
invokes your water-mother.
   When the green Earth will rise from hell
      like a night-lamp, on a wharf... (all-souls' repose).

9.19.23

92

A breeze leads the waves of flickering serpent-skin
    upstream, while the river flows south –
        folding an origami
        palimpsest, a pearl-lined mouth.
    That Hopewell sign, in Ohio – green undulation
  coiling toward the cosmic egg
of First Woman... *Voici.*
  Another Seine flows by the crag
    of Notre Dame, *mon âme... absolut américain.*

    The river in the mind glimmers. She sheds
        an upright ray from the horizon,
            swallowed by the sky.
        This water is transparent *raison*
    d'être – wells Hope with exactitudes,
  with Pythagorean splendor.
Note, by and by,
  her equal sign : the character
    of shared divinity (our dove-kissed heads).

    Throned in ancient limestone sediment
        the moving stream is motionless;
            her net of inborn truth
        enfolds its law of love and fairness
    with four agate threads, for Jonah's tent –
  a river of rivers (your heart).
Just so old *Toothy-Mouth*
  intones, recoils your happy start,
    America – so rich, so bitter. So repent.

                                        9.20.23

93

The prattling hubbub of the crowd grows quiet
  as the lights dim down. The empty stage
   is still. Outside
   the slapping paddle-wheels engage
 a twilight river's endlessness. Hamlet
steps out into a frozen Denmark.
And Ophelia has died.
 Peto's trompe-l'oeil *nature morte*
   is absinthe green, swamp green... (Ophelia's net).

 A flat green, on old painted boards –
  some craftsman's basement workbench.
    Ticket stubs (Ford's
    Theatre). That haggard mensch,
   wistful, glances from a small oval. No words.
  The cosmic tragedy is comic,
somehow – hordes
 of angry, manic wolves can't stick
   it to the shepherd... and *The End* is God's.

 The Magi on the road to Bethlehem
   listened to clip-clops, camel-thumps
   like paddle-wheels. The star
  was silent overhead. Bumps
 on a turtle's log, these wise men. Autumn
 drones with crickets and cicadas.
Ophelia looks far
 beyond this battlefield – her father's
   gazing down. Quiet at Gettysburg, Antietam.

9.22.23

94

Jackson was quick upon the steering wheel.
  Pilots must show themselves alive
    all hours, on the river –
    balance their keel upon an octave,
  threading the sinuous current... by feel.
What is Man, that Thou regard'st him?
Worming each serpent-quiver.
  So speak to me, strange hymn;
    let us have colloquy ensemble, O – Ophelia.

  Jessie Ophelia. Dark almond eyes
    beneath black hat – tall *fin-de-siècle*
      Paris elegance,
    in the ancient photograph. Grey shell
  of turtledove (grandfather's Quick surmise);
  great-great-grandmother, up
through faded reminiscence
  like a tortoiseshell, or agate cup.
    Whose whorl of springing voices wells... *surprise.*

  We know love is a fire of otherness
    like the subtle, fearsome river
      surging underneath
    our stubby tub. She is the *giver*,
  not the *taker* – each compassionate caress
  lifts up the boat (rudder to mast).
She will bequeath
  wisdom to pilots – Lincoln's quest
    for mercy, justice, Union. Turtle's kiss.

9.25.23

95

Lightning, thunder at the end of September.
  Rough wind. Heavy rain.
    I'm here, in the dark
  with flashlight (power's off again).
  They're shutting down the capital, remember –
in D.C. (distraught Columbia).
Divergent twain... Mark.
 A rivalry, Ophelia.
  You're mere colloquial – a leaf grown sere.

  Whilst Henry, the hammy hero, seeks his Grail.
    Abe Lincoln is his Fisher King –
      wounded in the head,
      O heart. Your canary will sing
    downstream, Cordelia... dove-wing, set sail!
  Coulombe, coulombe... your murmuring
outruns this masquerade.
  The rain that Paris Thursdays bring
    outshines all chivalry, in its chain mail.

  What is this cricket-mystery, O Lord?
    Who chirps out of the bottomlands
      like steadfast memory,
    immoveable and proud? *All hands
on deck.* The river flows past Jordan-ford;
  the fire will sear your heart, also.
Her whisper-gallery
  circuits a coracle – its glow
    accents your lamp, Psyche (soft turtle-word).

9.29.23

96

Nicolas of Cusa, *en voyage* from Byzantium
  was decked as if by lightning
    by a vision of God –
  whose incommensurable being
is pure *otherness*... a *Someone* beyond sum.
The sea, maroon and stormy, whorled
clouds, overhead
 into an hourglass figure; world-
  matrix, or enigma – pilgrim's game.

  Edgar Poe, too, had a strange vision –
   a giant wraith, in shrouds of mist,
    after a doomed voyage
   to Antarctica. An amethyst
  waterfall, like chain-mail, pierced by sun...
figure of Old Man *Okean*,
bearing a last message
 for humankind : *Return, return,*
  O ye forsaken ones! *Return to* UNION!

  In my whisper-gallery, that tarnished dome
   of lost Latrobe, in New Orleans
    doves flutter there
   small tongues of fire. Their orisons
  curve our horizons up to choirs of home.
 An acorn cornucopia
of coracles – where
 wellsprings spiral from Itasca
  and where *One* is love's *Equality*, calling... *Become.*

10.1.23

97

Latrobe's design for the Capitol dome
  hearkens back to Greece and Rome
    and further back, even –
  to each mud-brick simulacrum
  bending star-ward, to the gods' high home.
 His cypress box, beside his son,
almost Egyptian –
 and where the River, too, is done –
  will slide into the Gulf Stream's frothy foam.

  I found an agate, cut from Lake Itasca
   by no human hand. Beneath
    the grey-winged brow
   of *Dove-Woman*, ready to bequeath
  her flock of turtles to the Serpent-Masque –
 in which *Father of Waters* grapples *Father
of Lies*. And we know
  how emerald Agate topples Emperor;
   etched on her stone casket, the word : EQUALITÀ.

  Help me discern, reader, my own dark meaning!
   How human sheep are torn by wolves
    across blistered Earth...
   and how this wrestling-masque resolves
  depends upon each human conscience. Turning
 from our stony-hearted selves
to that river-morning –
 when hovering grey turtle-doves
  descend... lift us... wellspring divining!

               10.4.23

98

The rains come now, after a hot dry summer.
   Time unwinds slowly, from a spring
     like this long river
   strong and steady, unreturning.
 A massive sternwheeler from the Equator
like a wooden hurricane, threshes
upstream... like anti-matter,
 or a vision from Norwegian marshes.
   What shall we players play – on board, in thunder?

   Orpheus, aboard the Argo, keened *Eurydice*
     his wife, his life. The Fisher King
       languished in Memphis
     over his balcony, to hear her sing :
   his Milky Psyche of the galaxies – ETERNITY.
 Old Abe forded the river there
as well... his mistress
 Justice, throned on stone Siena chair
   was *Liberty*. Her lamp is lit – the play's to be.

   Now crickets thrum into October bronze;
     their sonorous reverberations sink
       beneath the fallen leaves.
     Hamlet steps out – to grieve, to think
   upon Ophelia's lambent grave. She mourns
 there still, in rippling echoes... her ship,
herself. The axle heaves
 against the grain. Mirrorrim skip
   on faery wings. *My father's seal*... (a gong resounds).

                                    10.6.23

99

My stream flows, constant as a metronome
  toward her high trumpet fanfare –
    Autumn's azure shore.
  From *portages de voyageur*
to New Orleans, October's wraith-kingdom
murmurs and rustles, underneath
of things that came before;
  those stones and booming bells bequeath
    intuitive harvestings... (heart's turtle-home).

Shades lengthen early in this light.
  Pious King Louis, on crusade
    boxed-in along the Nile
    cried – *Guilhem-le-Désert*! *M'aidez*!
  (Guillem, who had long ago abjured that fight).
  The Mississippi passes by.
The Arch (a campanile
 of air) shepherds infinite sky –
  Whose center is everywhere... whose call is flight.

               *

Love called Sant'Agata of Sicily;
each swelling dome lifts in her memory.
Each local mandala we shape, like ants
harks back to one most-intimate absence

our absent-minded present yet reveals –
bumping across this *Game of Spheres*, an aggie wheels.
The river floods its banks... the preacher dips
our heads. *Turtle-Dove* plummets – burns our lips.

               *

An unresting River-Serpent carves the earth;
   restless people carve the serpent
    for a sepulcher –
  some claustrophobic, water-closet
  Locked-Room Mystery. It is the Death
 we recognize, in autumn. All
our blind wars recur –
 echoing that whimsical leaf-fall.
  Yet still our pregnant planet groans toward birth.

  Be with me, Aggie – spinning, green-eyed orb!
   Sister to Psyche, Beatrice...
    cherished *Turtledove*...
   9-stringèd lyre of Sicily!
  Let your compassionate bloodstream absorb
 all nurses, firefighters, rape-
victims... Haunted love,
 draw near – mark this inscape :
  your wingèd turtleshell be our plumb-bob.

10.9.23

100

Come, full moon, round marble
over the black sea (vast and mournful).
Bring your green-eyed gravity to bear
on lonesome *us*... our windblown everywhere.

Doom keeps within your solitary crystal.

From adamant yearning comes the kiss of peace.
Come moon; come, Hermione – let innocence
trump guile. Let your *trompe-l'oeil* release
each prisoner's despair... (agate of Orleans).

*

In that consciousness beyond imagining,
our little world is just a blue-green aggie
ricocheting down galactic aisles – thumbing
through files (MURDER MOST FOUL). *Maggie,*

we hardly knew ye. Dry leaves from Camelot
encrypt a Newport wedding. Treasons plot.

One who dips his bread in the dish with me...
Guile follows gladness like a shadow. See
how the days decline, into November! Still
we'll bind these leaves – the stone winecup fill.

*

The number of the moon anchors an Ark
that's mirrored in the tides. Stone spires
of Thierry, at Chartres (long ago), embark
toward a sanction human liberty requires :

from *Union*, comes *Equality*... in *Love*.

Come Moon... come back, midsummer dream.
This tragic, too-familiar plot... redeem.
The cosmic nature of the human soul
is lent (by Mercy) from on high – and that is all.

10.10.23

101

The stream flowed here long before the imprint
   of my foolish foot. Of anyone.
      Black Elk traced
   a transparent octahedron –
index of primordial intent
to ask a blessing... smoke the pipe
of peace. The river laced
   her moccasin of clay – ripe
   epithalamium (sky-fundament).

This paradisal *glossolalia*
   of *animale compagnevole*
      must try *Siege Perilous* –
   where knees drop to ridgeway
   and *Jeanne d'Arc* flares like *Sant'Agata*;
   where *l'ancienne Amérique française*
out of forgetfulness
   midwives de Tocqueville... parlays
   étrange vert radieux – SANCTA MEMORIA.

You don't know why I'm talking like this.
   The fellowship of friendly Man
      depends upon a thorn
   beyond our ken – a heartfelt plan,
   ineffable and providential (*Miss-
is-Sippy* mystery). A Milky
Way. So join
   me, here – with Lincoln, *JFK*...
   with *MLK*. Black Elk – his crucifix.

10.13.23

102

Autumn's midpoint : soon fragile oak-leaves
  crumble like dry syllables.
    On Caribbean shores
  waves flash, immeasurable
into sunlit infinity – like sheaves
of wheat, scattered by Ocean River.
My ancient heart implores
 no more. A sabbath from *Forever*
  seeps from its wellspring; soul no more bereaves.

Love looms from elsewhere – unaccountable grace.
  I seek her center in this place
    like a blind man, listening;
  I sense the stream's relentless race
and yet some *J*-stroke's whorl impedes her pace.
Reverberations echo back –
mourning, remembering...
 and gather strength. Slow turtles track
  a mandala, atop their shells – an agate-face.

A Turtledove drifted to Jordan bank
  from above, from below... (familiar
    stranger). *Thou shalt love*
  the Lord your God, Jonah, with all your
heart, and soul, and mind – unto the brink
with all your steadfast strength of will
until that Turtledove
 nestles within, and shines there, still –
  lifting your drownèd IMAGO (Thanksgiving, Hank).

10.15.23

103

Your elegant sketch, Benjamin, for the Capitol dome –
  I can only conjure it, like an echo
    round the whisper gallery.
  You, a bleached wash in the Bayou –
Everyman, Unknown Soldier – tossed into foam
 like some no-count gray pebble;
blind, like me;
  face hewn like massive Inca marble
    from Andes peaks (Abe Lincoln palindrome).

The architecture of collective purpose
  reaches toward a trim proportion
    – sturdy, seaworthy,
    graceful and free. True Union
of the word and thing, the mind and heart – a Paradise
of some pilot's devising (Jonah
rowing home, maybe).
  Who rises from the mandorla –
    the womandoor, the womb-door... (*Rio del Espiritus*).

The visible world, a spiral hieroglyph
  or labyrinth, reverberates
    with unseen whisper-waves –
    unexpected shipmates,
  their impetuous embrace. Into the Gulf
we go, to glimpse your smiling grail :
green stone, with architraves
  of four rivers... beyond the pale
    of admirals (like Santa Cruz de Tenerife).

10.16.23

104

The golden bird chirps like a constant cricket
  happy in his constancy,
    like Constans at Hagia Sophia.
    Like a mechanical Agatha Christie...
  whodunnit, then? *Murder Most Fowl*, Becket.
 That Union man (in *The Irishman*) –
a gyrating Pandora,
  doorkeep to the infernal basin –
    summons the wrath (beneath *Macbeth* chess-set).

  Our mob simmers with resentment. Jordan,
    the Prince, wrestles with himself
     to bring it all to boil –
    this pantomime of grief and pelf...
  la condition humaine. Chilly echo-span
of iron – joining John Wilkes Booth,
Oswald... Hamilton's foil,
  Benedict Arnold... the mob, forsooth,
    calls for *Barabbas* – brazen *trompe-l'oeil* twin.

  The Cricket of Peace is a cicada, Jonah –
    humming like a swarm of bees
     from another, happier
    dimension. The dream of Socrates,
  the scapegoat shepherd's kingdom... Louisiana?
 A child's playground, near Camelot
where the Grail is *someone*
  (Imogen – the Lady of Shalott?).
    Turtledove swims in the deep (a pumice mandorla).

10.19.23

125

105

The pilot said to me : *After a while*
  the river gets inside of you.
   You always ride the current –
  even on shore. That flow
  gets in your blood, becomes your blood. You smile!
 But it's the truth. I looked away
downstream – toward St.
  Louis, New Orleans, the Delta...
  and the sea. O Lord, pilot my soul!

  Shakespearean players clamber up topside
   to fling duelling soliloquies.
    To prance, preen, prink
   and garner laughter – thoughtful tears
  (backlit by twilight vastness, thunderhead).
  October maples flame the hills;
Earth lifts her cup, to drink
  our Fisher King – his vow fulfills.
   Ford's Theatre is everywhere (*Everyman's Regicide*).

  That Irishman, with his redhead brother
   pushed back against brute force,
    vain thespian guile.
   A higher justice fixed their course –
  ineffable equality of law (*Do unto other*
as you love your own). O human
fellowship – *si compagnevole*!
  There is the cosmic congregation,
   my friend : *Do justice on this Earth, your mother.*

10.20.23

106

A month past Equinox, this rickety gazebo
   rhymes with my time of life,
     the season of farewell
   and yellow leaves. Primeval strife
  is for young champions of April – Zorro,
St. George, Zarathustra...
harrowing each hell
  where Iago preys on Desdemona;
   devious Milan haunts bookish Prospero.

   I stroll along the river, with a heavy heart
    that should be featherweight, my dove –
     be with me, Mater
    Ma'at! My academic grove
  has grown pedestrian, despite my art.
  Pedantic courtiers disclaim
the hour's getting later,
  while that dragon's tongues of flame
   scorch the paddleboat of state with every dart.

   But this is not the venerable Nile
    and I am not the Mississippi
     though I stream that way.
    The river is a sprite, maybe.
  Come, Ariel – lift your campanile
of double rainbows in the air!
Miranda's here to play!
  The chess game of innocence is where
   the Magi meet their match (her infant smile).

10.23.23

107

Slowly, down the lofty oaken nave
  of East River Road, I walked.
    Past my grandfather's house,
   whose ruddy bricks demarked
his high cheekbones – their steep conclave
like the river-cliff. That Longfellow place
next door – where a church-mouse
  named *Magnus* twirled (with cheesy grace)
  Osiris's baton... over his river-grave.

  Where, then, Servius, is the Grail – and what?
   Is it? Some Camel cigarette
    for Jack? Across the street,
   the Brain Science Center is wet
with October rain. Some kind of nut –
acorn? – rides Frisbee's quantum kayak
over the falls... complete
  surrender to the flow, Psyche
                    (*forget-*

  me-knot). Hamlet's on the parapet.
   He longs to see his father's ghost –
    closer, closer, someone
   whispers in his ear. *O Most*
High, condescend to descend... your host
parlays eternal life! He dealt
her, once – Persephone,
  Jessie Ophelia; sweet Delta net
   lifted to airy awe (Gate to the West).

                    10.24.23

108

Ripe autumn light molts off so quickly, now.
  Shaky *Henry Duplex*, late
    of subtle Cecil St.
    fixes his eye on a Spanish plate
  of clay. A swollen Minotaur curves low
his coiled bullhorn – so serpentine,
this prancing brute!
  Beside a handmade peasant scene –
    a solemn-sweet *Last Supper*, out of Mexico.

  Old bookish sot, I dote like Prospero
    upon my mother's figurines.
      Whom doth the Grail serve?
    Serves perfect Beauty, dear Beguines!
  Oozing from the *Light-of-Lights*, like myriad mellow
oak-leaves, waltzing their sarabande
across a cosmic swerve;
  like JFK, in old Rhode Island
    signing up VISTA volunteers (to serve tomorrow).

  The wind grows cold, the days grow short. The Spirit
    whispers from an arctic sky... murmurs
      goodbye. Soul and body
    must divide, someday – these wars
  a pantomime of *General Death* (that great despot).
  Yet the Grail is a perfect turtleshell
(charity's remedy);
  hope, courage, wisdom swell
    like fountains from Itasca well – snow-crystal bright.

                              10.25.23

109

That dented ball of Nicolas of Cusa
  retards its rolling, slowing down.
    Dangerously close
  to winter's vortex, and our own –
a snowy stasis (spinning planet's *Via*
Crucis). Both my legs are weak.
Cracks in my knees
 like Mr. Grail King, up the creek...
  bloodstream like frozen lake (his *Last Hurrah*).

  In green grass the other day, I found a mushroom.
   Unknown Soldier. Oval helmet
    sagging like an egg
   of Mycenaean bronze (with net
 of milky cadmium). Dragon's teeth loom
out of the ground... an alphabet
from *Alph* to *Beg* –
 from *Maecenas* to wounded vet –
  from casque to cask to casket (narrow room).

  The green rays gather to a red brainwave.
   That infant (like François Villon)
    swings on homemade gibbet,
   handsome guillotine. He's the one!
 Our missing Inca Lincoln (*vale*, brave)
framed by the arkwright of the Earth
for one *trompe-l'oeil* exhibit :
 hieroglyph of *justice* (breath
  of light). Its heart is mercy, courage, love.

              10.30.23

110

The flow below the ridge reflects November
  in its still, brown shimmering,
    flecked with spiderwebs
    of silver-gray. Everything
  curls back into this bronze-gold amber –
shaggy ink cap, Argo helm;
Mycenaean plebs
  airlifted from St. Louey's realm
    on shaggy manes, like lawyers' wigs... remember?

Mushroom cloud, or cloudy mushroom? Shakespeare's
  happy cup we shall imbibe
    aboard the *Pegasus*,
    my almond-eyed Sea Scout – your tribe
  of nurses, firefighters... your casket full of tears.
  The Grail is matrix of a stone
communion. Psyche's
  a dove, Jonah – *Jeanne, Joan*...
    her ark's an agate gateway (azure spheres

of fire). Jackson Quick, the river-pilot...
  Abraham Lincoln... your flickering icon
    is already gone.
    Sleep-sickness, mutters Charon;
  your wintry photograph's a *nature morte*.
  Float me back to Itasca now,
Psyche; only your agate sun
  is lamp for me. Dark river, flow –
    deep *Rio del Espiritu Santo* (your whisper-mote).

11.1.23

111

Here I am, late, on All Souls' Night.
  Observe the criss-cross dent in the crown
   of that shaggy ink cap
   from Mycenae. We are all one
  in your almond eye, Psyche – we all take flight
 out Narragansett smoke-hole, or the dome
in Benjamin's sketch-map
  (his turtledove – distraught *Coulombe*).
   Renew your mind; she's born to set it right.

  Mind and spirit are the earth's Brain Science.
   All is personal, down to the core.
    All's figures, foolish
    Feste (not-so-foolish). Tell me more!
   Your brook's a serpentine and tacit sense
 of time, passing – 'sblood, flowing –
Redemption, not so schoolish
  but an inescapable inscape – deep-going
   ubi caritas est vera spring (green radiance).

  And how this came to be, the unknown soldier
   bears her witness, lastingly –
    moreso than bronze helmet
   your sheltering wings, Psyche
  are aegis-aerie from Ariel. There,
there! Your Turtle surfaces –
your arc, Jehanne, your jet!
  And this *Spirit of St. Louis*
   (Paris-bound) no bias stains. Dove, share!

        11.2.23

112

Guy Fawkes – the Fox – the *faux* guy –
   set a keg beneath Parliament
    and would eliminate the King;
   would (like a reverse trumpet)
  sliver his silver, in a guileful way –
 turning the words against themselves;
tarnishing everything
 with shifty blame (the very evil
  he so delves out of himself).

  The naked Child, in dire extremity
   curls like spring into the well
    of milky headwaters –
   almond wombdoor... turtleshell...
  ark preceding all our misery;
 receding back to *Dreamtime*
where its matrix mutters
 of an *Ocean River*... Jonah's hymn
  the Whale taught her (scared *Enaree*).

  This feminine French shadow of Louisiana
   sets her lips against my ear
    like *Dove*, continually.
   November rain, in the year's gutter
  pours like Thursday... like a Paris manna –
 bitter, rich (impoverished villain).
Your bell sounds deeply
 in my heart, *amie*. Sing it again.
  Equality-Union-Concord (*eucharistia*).

              11.5.23

113

Beneath cool air, anemic sunlight
  I walk along (inside this agate
    of November). Brown
  the river, brown the leaves, that
  flicker bits of gold, green, scarlet...
as the wind lofts every falling leaf
into soft sprightly swoon –
  scattering... folding into sheaf
    one *lento* tarantella (winter's *fête*).

When hearth is full of heat, and mind is light
  bronze helmets turn to shaggy manes,
    shaggy Shakespeare's-eyes
  of Inca happiness. Those octahedrons
of Black Elk are *Pegasus*, in Shetland flight,
and up their narrow, deltahedron
agateway, we rise –
  with milky King, and Abe Lincoln,
    and redhead Grail-splitter (*Union*, tonight).

Haunted by the abyss of hollowness
  your soul, your conscience, lonely Jonah
    touches the crossroad spine
  of Life – your smiling Beatrice
from eternal fountains... emerald radiance!
Black Elk's Euclidean eucharist,
Thanksgiving pine –
  that narrow path to Sabbath rest;
    one spark of heart-fire showering our nest.

11.7.23

114

November sun is low. The Fire-Worm flits
  beneath the surface waves of guile,
   their fickle ripplings.
  He foments faction in the guppy school,
 to magnify himself – tear them to bits.
 Yet from thy Bottomland matrix
of all wellsprings...
 my *Dolphin-Sis*, my swanning Beatrix
  breaches the Gulf (flinging galactic castanets).

  Her *Ocean* channel's narrow, and obscure.
   Ophelia, Hermione and Prospero
    will drown their salty book
   to show the way : *you must let go
 all things*. Dispossession is redemption's door.
 And in the agate of her mandorla
4 streams form *cirque* :
 around that stone casket of Golgotha
  we sense one hearth-beat... streaming sure.

  Grandfather's house is on the River Road.
   On either side are bridges. Down the way
    spans Berryman's (a third).
   Two younger brothers leapt, nearby
  from each; and cousin Julie met the flood
 beneath the Golden Gate (lifetime
ago). *Only say the word*,
 Juliet. Where pigeons, seagulls climb
  I'll taste your salt... lift me to everlastinghood.

11.8.23

115

My numbers cannot spell this golden light
  that filters through the late year's grave.
    But I can fingerpaint
    its wayless way – a river-nave
  whose spirals wind, unwind – loose, tight –
out of the curvature of sky
until you sense it : silent,
  faint... yet firm enough to fly
    our hearts into its headwaters (beyond insight).

We work our way toward what we cannot see
  through rest. Vast *Ocean River*
    drowses on downstream
    within your dream, Eurydice –
  you hear her voice bring everything to be
within one lonesome whistle-stop
small-planet scheme :
  one green-earth flute, with flowery top.
    O taste the cosmic honey of his galaxy!

My old Gray Lady there is adamant.
  She's throned on agate-circled stone.
    She's midwived every man
    and woman... folds them into one
  heartworn embrace. That's Love's sole talent :
lambent above *grande, pacifique* prairie,
Equality's her sun –
  and with such concord all reality
    groans toward Union (Abraham's event).

11.9.23

116

... and Jessie was a dark and lovely branch
  of Jackson Quick (her mother's father).
   River-pilot, unknown
  soldier... died aboard a side-wheeler
at Vicksburg. Later, Liz Quick would launch
a restaurant, in St. Louis
 and snag a giant green
  sea-turtle, up from New Orleans;
   quick-witted Jessie O. would help make lunch.

The riverboats still plied the Mississippi,
  up and down, and traveling players
   played along. Liz
  Friedheim loved all Shakespeare's –
Cleopatra Desdemona... Jessie Ophelia
were her daughters, and the Bard's.
Whose skull be this,
 crowner, gravedigger? Beauregard's,
  milord – the little black frenchman. Gone to sea.

Lincoln, and the milky King, and JFK
  have slipped downstream, as well. It is
   day after Armistice.
  Your grail, Ophelia, coos
like a turtleshell... your weedy coracle's
my oracle. Our tapped-out soldier's
gone to his almond rest –
  and through that oval at St. Louis
  (swallows' airy tomb) he takes to the sky.

11.12.23

117

My figures are but shadows of your numbers
  Blessèd One. Benevolent nine Muses
   bend thy autumn light
   into a fold, that unconfuses –
  into a radiant flock of spectra (rainbows
raying from your *Ocean Stream*).
So orient my night
  toward Day : oar this Black Sea trireme
   entre Byzantium, Jerusalem... (sea-showers).

  That granite Ojib-Jonah woman at Itasca
   rain J-stroking through her hair
    points out the turtle path
   downriver (rowing toward her azure
  Ocean lair). It is a native masque
in New Orleans – when Joan of Arc
leaps beyond wrath
  and Cusa's chunkey-ball hits Mark
   Twain lightly on the brain... (*only* ASK HER).

  My Hippo's blue, and metropolitan,
   Augustine : inked across my skin
    like Queequeg's coffin
   or *Book of the Dead* (the shroud is thin
  this time of year). Listen, Jonathan :
  Jonah's a woman (Beatrice,
or Ophelia). *When*
  kindling sparks Dunce Inane (eh,
   trumpster smoke)... *your* DOVE *shall reign.*

11.13.23

118

I lit my torch and searched for you, Psyche;
  up and down the riverbank,
    my night's Big Muddy.
  But couldn't find you. Not at the Bank
 nor in the Forum... not in the turbulent city.
   Meanwhile, a little poison puffball
 swelled an orange bloody
  whale of outraged Mammon (all
    our sin ballooning to one *trompe-l'oeil* Deity).

  Sweet ripples in the stream of time
    make poetry. But my clepsydra
      is a water-thief;
     his crown-wheel but a replica,
    his heartbeat plummeting past primal crime
   full fathom five, father.
Commander-in-Chief,
  maestro to all our tragic bother,
    comic relief... (Ariel's late romance-rhyme).

  Tick-tock. That Everyman (serrated soldier
    on his jagged rack) is serving time –
      it's criminal, your
     Majesty. Take him (lame
   Irish ray) to Camelot – his grail's your
  agate, Crow. Time speeds the plow.
*Work, for the late hour
  fades to darkness quickly, now.*
    Your heart's in your son's hands, Lord. *Heart, share.*

11.15.23

119

From the proud parapet, the river far below
  shimmers like smooth serpent,
    sunlit constancy
  of silver pennies, never spent.
  Each human being is a leggèd river, so –
a Nile, a walking Ouroboros;
a two-ft. Mississippi-
  snaggled *Toothy-Mouth*, in grass
    disguise – clocked unknown soldier... (see him go).

  Henry, Henry, teetering on the ledge –
    seared jingle-jungle heart
      encased in icebound
    crown-wheel – each epileptic start
  ticks back, a toxic tocsin... needs a dredge.
O them wheels in wheels, Ezekiel!
Feet on the ground
  sad Nicolas looks up... to smile!
    Venn rainbows bend from *Ocean River's* edge!

  Ouroboros is only Milky Way.
    And the Mystery King who plays each trump
      returns to where she's been
    always : green *Agata*, nursing a lump
  in every chest. A casket for *That Day*,
a grail of flowing river-tears...
stone zen garden
  that weathers, like your *Game of Spheres*,
    Cusanus. Graceful stands your tree, Ojibwe.

11.19.23

120

The River says : Love runs so deep…
  beneath this noise my surface makes.
   Full fathom five
  the wind whispers, a feather takes.
 Lift up your heart, child. Do not weep.
 His hand upon my molten brow
kept me alive –
 that iron crown-wheel of tomorrow
  rims a milky Gateway. *Feed my sheep.*

 Thus be my Mississippian clepsydra –
  a mode of escapement? Undulating
   serpent-skin? (Hopewell,
   Hopewell.) *Angryman's treasoning!*
 Harry Mazda cries. *And from Cahokia
 to now, the crossroad of St. George
beckons – O Holy Grail!*
 Our hero-dreams… only the forge
  where souls are hammered into gold *finalità.*

 Absalom, my son, my son! Your saga
  underlying every psalm –
   a family betrayal,
   trumping every public shame.
 J-stroke upstream, toward St. Agata;
 that Turtle-Woman at the source
will hear your trial.
 Will weigh your heart's muddy remorse,
  and (maybe) lift you to the Gulf. *Alleluia.*

11.20.23

121

These figures in a Mississippi shadow-play,
　like Noh, or Neva ships a-sail
　　toward Black Sea
　　clarity – salt in the barrel
of your conscience, Henry Hale. *If not today,*
Horatio... ripeness is all.
The readiness, you see.
　Prithee, Sasha, take my pistol.
　Ophelia lies there... *et voici ma clé.*

　My glossolalia, like muddy stream
　　I would refresh. The human conscience
　　　is remote pole star,
　　　and yet your pilot is a *mensch*
　(sweaty, bloody). Afterbirth (*crème*
de la crème) of *Theotokos* –
adamant loin-sire,
　lion of Judah. She who wears
　　the galaxies... (one wellspring beam).

　Psyche... Brain Science... agate veil...
　　Shakespeare's happy cupola –
　　Anna Akhmatova's
　　Hopewell (Nadezhda)... *et voilà* :
　your *syestra-douve* becomes my humble Grail.
　Your headwaters, Jonah, my globe.
Your spring (Itasca's)
　welcomes Benjamin Latrobe –
　　his homely dome, *Coulombe*, sprang from the whale.

11.20.23

122

O Man – meek humpty-dumpty Hobo clod...
  Unknown Soldier, in your baseball cap
    marked VERITAS –
  forked lightning draws the thunderclap
      ***
follow that serpent, wiser than you
inching through dust
  with sinuous humility; for the high blue
    dome hides remote heavens... past flesh and blood.

  Yet thou, *Hagia Sophia*, art nearer than near.
    We are heart-murmurs in your womb;
      if only we bend low
    into the grass of this April tomb,
  we'll hear you singing beyond wrath, and the fear
  of death; we'll taste clear spring-water
of universal Law;
  we'll meet the *Turtledove*, your daughter –
    walk with her toward *Liberty* (penny so dear).

  Beauty on Earth is evanescent, yet nothing else
    so beautiful as this. The green King
      of Camelot was slain;
    so the magnanimous Fisher King
  of our Republic; so the milky King of paradise.
  Yet what they lived for was a *Love*
Supreme – will come again!
  The Mississippi of the *Turtledove*
    is green *Rey* – evergreen... (blue Gulf she swells).

        11.21.23

123

It was only a breath of pale gold light
  the sky exhaled across this day;
    one revived ember
  in the twilight of the year; one ray.
  Thanksgiving waits, on the other side of night –
our planetary troubled sleep;
I am a loyal member
  in memoriam (Jack's journey to the deep).
  Time stopped; we mourned the sense of being right.

When I was young, I was a VISTA man
  in Providence; Jack's birthday was my own.
    Now I'm almost a ghost
  as much as he... and yet the groan
  of laboring good will, I understand.
  The builders of this world, in love
and innocence, from coast
  to coast, frame one alcove –
  bonded by human dignity, in *Union*.

The Destroyer has no form, no shape.
  He only comes to denigrate,
    divide – he hates the light.
  His heart is theft. His means are great.
  And delicate *Columbia* he longs to rape.
  And yet Jack Quick, the pilot, still
recalls his father's fight –
  to stand with Abraham's good will
  in Vicksburg... shed the martyr's ruby grape.

11.22.23

124

I walked along the River Road this morning
    past my grandparents' brick house
      a few blocks beyond
    that bridge, where JB's life would close.
  He danced an Irish fugue of hope and mourning.
  I hear his piercing pennywhistle
through this fog of despond;
  I hear the tonic of de Tocqueville
    ring : *la République Humaine* a-dawning.

  A melodious undertone in French-American
    with washboard bass, harmonica...
      Rhode Island Cajun
    (℅ Roger Williams, via
    Eddie Coke). All pure Parisian
  Republican – *Liberté*,
Égalité...
  o'ershadowed by that *Charité*
    straight out of Thierry, at Chartres *(trans-humaine).*

  A stream of water flows, straight from the heart
    of iron Earth. A rusty, copper-
      green, and living water –
    fountain of one prophet-pauper
  (unknown soldier). Spring where every part
  becomes whole again. That Jordan measure,
equitable matter :
  love thy Maker, and your neighbor.
    With magnanimity – where rivers start.

11.23.23

125

Now the feasting is over. The planet fades
   beneath its brown blanket, toward sleep.
      An old child turns away
      from pastimes, toward the spirit's keep.
   Each person is a gyroscope – cascades
along a tightrope, drawn by lodestone
(agate gateway)
   toward Love's arching capstone :
      warm heart... infant king of winter shades.

There is one sabbath rest that sets you free.
   One eye upon Osiris-boat
      from night to day,
      one oval turtle-dovecote
   chalice (table-round geometry).
The crown-wheel of the human heart –
its play-within-a-play.
   So put aside all servile art
      and cross this Jordan to eternity.

 On a wrinkled wall, in a monks' refectory
   of a bookish Duke's Milan... palms
      tender poker hands –
      flickering guile, offering alms
   unto their fatal Lamb, unceasingly.
They love him. So do we.
The Turtle understands.
   Our *Brave New World* reality
      spins like a top – with tragic gravity.

                              11.24.23

126

Today we were driving east on Highway 7
  Excelsior, Hopkins, St. Louis Park
   toward Mendelssohn
  when some invisible ray, or spark
  beamed from my heart – took me back home again.
 Westward, along that trolley line
where my life began.
 And a wave of adoration (Proustian)
  welled up... green ray of setting sun.

  The hollow heart pursues its hollow things.
   To erase, with envy, what it loves
    in vain – greed, pride,
   fraud – dominion that it craves
  to the destruction of all innocent beings
 and good makings. Yet there's a thread,
an invisible guide
 stems from the heart – rises from the dead;
  a *Love Supreme*... (mourning dove that sings).

Consider dying Benjamin Latrobe
burying his son, in New Orleans.
His radiant marble curvature remains
in Washington – his mind issued a globe.

Thy classic grace... only an agate lamp.

Our works are elegant, but not so vast
as photons arrowed by the human heart.
That Orphic *chelys* of Apollo's art
urns azure Gulf (slight Delta mast).

So we meander, elliptical, toward the sea.

Mississippi is a rugged beast –
a forlorn Cleopatra.
Cleopatra Desdemona (feast
for jaundiced eyes, Ophelia). I see,
Susanna. That righteous son of Jesse,
bathing Bathsheba,
is but a man (poet, maybe)
and Lent precedes Mardi Gras, in Galilee.

The children of America deserve
a Lincoln *logos* – innocent
as snakeskin, wise
as doves. A complex, decent
civilization. Unbeholden to the swerve
of greed, or brutal violence.
We come in human guise,
guys... *coraggio*, resilience
and truthfulness. *Whom does the Grail serve?*

11.25.23

127

Who goes there? cries the Elsinore watchman.
  Mark the twin Pegasi –
    how they cross the stream!
  Your father's ghost was in my eye,
  St. Louis – where the *strong brown god* began
to widen. Speed more turbulent.
Life is a dream,
  the Polish prince declared. Sent
    to break brittle hearts... and let *coraggio* in.

  Picture a small, green, Ice Age basin.
    Glacial moraine – pine-ringèd cirque.
      In the grass there grows
    a bronze-gold salience, circled
  with cloud... a spectral ink-cap (shaggy mane).
  Imagine a confluence of waters –
some clepsydra-*kairos*
  (whose Columbian pathos endures).
    Vast earth enfolds man's bronze dominion.

  That Turtle-woman at the headwaters
    displaced the Eagle with a Jonah-
      dove. It was the sabbath-
      day. Rest now, Deborah –
  Joan of Arc – from all your fierce labors.
  I have no wrath, I have no wrath,
the Ghost-king sings. *Selah.*
  Not male nor female on this path –
    but *Union*, in *Equality* (alpine flowers).

                              11.27.23

128

If the pilot's blind, and babbles incoherently
  why would you paddle downstream with him?
   You're here – it is what it is.
   The Mississippi floats a skim
of ice today. *A shaggy ink cap is the key.*
Its iron horseshoe curvature
might give us pause...
  all that's left of one brave creature.
  Unknown Soul, of U.S.G.? Say – can you see?

   Unknown soldier. Buried in quicklime
   outside Vicksburg. Grant's Tomb,
    his New York sepulcher.
   A marble fountain in the gloom.
  All cryptic memory's a kind of crime
against Time – lifting the canoe
like an ark, to hover
  upright... crosswise... to the Blue;
   over the river, like an airborne rhyme.

   Whirlpool... elliptical orbit... mandorla
   of mandorlae. The Magdalen,
    missing at Last Supper...
   Martha, your sister has chosen
the good part, which shall not be taken from her.
  The wintry mirror of the river
shimmers toward her
  goal. Your dream draws near.
   The Gulf is azure beyond gold (*Eternità*).

                    11.28.23

129
to Juliet Ravlin, 1952-1971

A poker deck of years, dear Juliet,
  since (plummeting from the Golden Gate)
   you ended everything.
   They're finishing a safety net
  at last. Too late, sweet cuz... too late.
 It's been a year of weeks, in years;
a house of cards, slipping
 across green baize – a bay of tears.
  Men's busy games mow down a green quiet.

  And life's November brings a brown detachment.
   Let it not mean indifference.
    Our lonely minds
   mirror all beauty (heartfelt sense
  no man's an island). Iron arcs are bent
 from shore to shore. The seagull's cry
far echoes binds.
 And Life, which tends merely to die,
  returns to life... immortal sacrament.

  Dear J. Ophelia, our safety net is torn
   by callous malice. Springs are not born
    to drown – heart's River
   guides our boats to solid haven.
  Shades of a marble dome in Washington
 extend an oblong, curving ray,
out from its green quiver
 through a vast, airy Gateway –
  calm rainbow, adamant and fair. Human.

11.29.23

130

The last day of November. The Spanish bull
　(in the Cretan plate) has been gored
　　by a green flag – looks up
　skyward, smiling (his own Ford
　Theatre). The Black Sea sighs... brimful
of emptiness, darkness. Salt
is Hippocrene stirrup;
　is fire, is good. *Have salt*
　　amongst yourselves, and be at peace (old mule).

Out of the sea, Perdita, Hermione...
　out of the sea came dove-winged
　　Aphrodite. Psyche...
　we hardly knew ye. Orpheus pinged
　taut cat-guts of the sail (*Enaree*,
wounded by womanhood – cowardly
loin) until Eurydice
　surfaced at last... breaching the lee
　　like infant hurricane. *Turtledove... bee!*

The Redemption has already happened, he wrote (*Pushkin*
　and Scriabin). This green ukulele
　　of the slough is breeding
　fireflies... light spectral arks;
　its knot of Lincoln is a *logos*-Union,
overflowing joy – its grail
only a bleeding
　cup of wine – a coracle
　　of floating wheat (a spark of singing grain).

11.30.23

131

The pilot on the broad, calm river
  sounds his agate plumb in peace.
    His stone compacts the weight
    of all the solid heaviness
  of things, across the universe. The sliver
of his line, like some *tromba marina*
hums its wavy transit
  of the river's *lento moderato*...
    one string singing through all things forever.

  I think of my father, a little farther off.
    Where I can see him, in the air's
      transparent distance.
    Watch how his gentle eye explores
    the world he loves, the play of dawning life.
  That look, that thought, are almost weightless –
unlike my own dense
  infant gravity. His tenderness.
    Flint-spark. Equality. Pythagorean proof.

  The model of perfection is a sketch toward truth,
    a way. Proved in the suffering arms
      of compassionate *Agape* –
    anchor of love against all harms.
    Infinite invisible light-rays arrow forth
  each morning – subtle, seamless web
forming one Gateway,
  hoisting one safety net. Ephebe,
    cast off. This agate plumbs our floating berth.

                    12.1.23

132

Those August evenings, when your mother would take us
all
 to that lily pool, by the Japanese Garden
  ringed by rhododendron
  for the festival of paper lantern-
 boats. A hundred paper hats, set sail
into the looming dusk. Such frail
bright sparks of sun!
 Across the dark back of Night Whale...
 your memory-sky (flutter-whirr, familial).

 We are all refugees from Paradise.
  We've all been driven from our homes
   by violence and fraud,
   fanatic hate. The forlorn kingdoms
  of the dispossessed... but dreams and promises.
 The ground? A flimsy coffin-boat
of tears – beseeching God
 to save us (from a sea of salt).
  Only a lofty feather-word can dry our eyes.

 In the depths of the museum, the Root Collection
  of ceramic art rests in silence.
   Loving hands cupped
  these delicate contraptions... with a sense
 stronger than force, beyond conception.
 We dwell in this translucent ark
as one; we've supped
 with strangers, lifted lights in dark.
  Agape is its peaceful plumb – pumice of reconciliation.

            12.2.

CODA

Our piñata was a particolored bull
   of *papier-maché*, with a tin voice-box
     that bellowed, loud.
   The kids took turns giving it whacks
  with a broom, 'til it exploded – chock-full
 of lightweight chocolate doubloons,
foiled in paper gold.
  Our ship was stalled between lagoons.
   The games gave pleasure (so much time to kill).

The grownups, in the stateroom, disagreed
   about the wisdom of our Captain.
     We're on a Ship of Fools,
   some said. *Takes one to know one*,
  some replied. Some even bruised and bled
 (a bit, anyway) over opinions...
no one knew the rules
 of Maritime Law in those regions.
   Someone proposed we sing the A.A. Creed.

That drew a laugh. You bet. Jackie thought
   she spied a rainbow over the bow
     – but it was a sundog.
   The sky grows dark and heavy, now.
   Thunder, lightning flashes – close to the boat.
 We thought of that splintered piñata...
was God an angry mug?
 Our mast (whorled in cumulo-strata)
   had vanished. S.O.S.... *What hath Man wrought?*

*

A scapegoat : it's a convenient solution.
  Somebody will have to pay
    for all our hot brute strength
    as a people... stolen by Time. No delay!
  Release *Bar-Abbas* – we want the *Son of Man*!
  These iron rings are never broken –
stretch him all his length.
  Say, innocent shepherd, Holy One –
    where is your Wisdom now (tormented Brain)?

  Now the *Beast from the Sea* shall surface, full of bull.
    He will restore our mighty kingdom
      with a single finger-point –
      multiplied across the spectrum
    by a thousand hands, a thousand decks... all
  dealing out blind wrath to foes!
Denmark is out of joint.
  There is no peace. (Ophelia knows...
    keening from the bottom of her salted well).

  And though we lose faith in our God, our neighbor
    yet we shall worship our floating Bull.
      His *papier-maché* is bright,
      his horns are bold, his shoulders swell
    with rage... big Hercules! No one is stronger.
  The answer to all our enemies
is force, is might!
  His hammer slays their circuiting shadows...
    dusk falling on a blood-red sea. O Victory!

*

Hot and angry in Angola, in this prison
   of ire, of lead – *Goodnight, Irene*
     Goodnight, Irene...
   sometimes I would take a great nation
  right down to the River, and drown again –
 drown our sorrows in that stream.
Goodnight, Dove-Gal,
 goodnight, sweetmilk... I'll see you in that beam
   of pine-green light (your agate lamp, St. Jeanne).

   Peaceful runs the river now, beneath the willows.
    Passing, unceasing, clear and constant.
     Here I would hang up
    your plumbline, knotted at the point
   around its weight of whorling curlicues –
 suspended there, like adamant.
One cup of fellowship.
  Your peace, Irene, is meek, benevolent...
   attuned to justice... like a lambent rose.

   Shalom, shalom. The stream flows on.
    Her source and mouth are fused in one.
     A bridge, a floating arc,
    an octave over harsh division –
   Concord and Equality, lifted to Union.
  The knot of human and divine
is sure – *twain, mark*!
  Atlantis rising, through Ariel-passion –
   new Bertha Friedheim song? *Amen, amen.*

              *

The arrows of an absinthe-green dolour
  are fanged, and serpentine – they rhyme
   with absence, and the greed
    of hungry kids (asleep, sometime).
  So force of malice struck our Man of Eire.
Johnny, we hardly knew ye...
we watched you bleed.
  Your aching spin molded our eye
    of hurricanes... tears of a VISTA volunteer.

   Charisma of a well-loved heroine.
    A chosen one (*rizz, rizz*)
     who steps into the fray
     mistakenly... a gentle Beatriz;
   Isaac's angel, and Abe Lincoln –
dressed to the nines (yeast
of the Muses' roundelay).
  Our building is a welded feast
    bonded like iron (floating *Constitution*).

   Your dreams whisper a sultry dialogue.
    Like rain in the Delta, summer
     (seedling decalogue) –
    but snow and ice now, come December.
   Somehow, the prow of happiness (through fog).
  They try to destroy it, sad children!
They do not mean to clog
  the arteries of Mrs. Sippy, son.
   Just azure blues – out of a salty bog.

*

They don't call M *Big Muddy* for nothing.
  My Coda is in morse code.
   An oblique conversation –
  post-regal fishing dude,
  mostly talking to himself. Wheezing
 with the monotonous current
down to its destination
  (gulp) – the Gulf. Your never-unspent
  prodigal slide, Walt! Trombones thing.

  Mr. Bones thing. Ham's in the crow's nest
   yammering his frayed lines...
    immoral mortal panic.
   Help him down please, friends!
  St. Anthony Falls – lonely place
 for a haywire hayseed's grail quest.
Baptism ain't no picnic
 in a fireplace. Be my guest,
  dear *Rio della Holy Ghost* – and bring Grace!

  And when the heart brims like a Celtic cauldron
   and green-eyed Irene is babbling
    her fortuitous falls
   (Minnehaha to you) – *Mirabile!*
  That spell-blind pilot-poet comes into his own
 like shark-tamer in disguise
(him *Heal-All* heal
 all heels). *Mississippi Surprise!*
  That big stern wheeler's a tricycled Master Plan.

*

Ironic how iron can prove irenic.
  The freight train is a friendly beast,
   rumbling across the bridge
  (river below). Black Elk points East.
 The train-horn hoots. In Memphis, MLK
on his last fatal day
helps lift the Garbage
 Union, on their justice way.
  Sweet labor rises with the sun. *Shalom*, I say.

There's deadly feuding at the Capitol.
  Parties have patented what's best.
   Meanwhile the plangent light
  of evening sounds. Black Elk points West.
 Those rose, mauve, azure veins will swell
one lucid radius, orthogonal –
one emerald flight;
 a signal from a fading dome (one fond farewell).

The Norway pine outside my window stands
  calm as a topmast in its berth,
   or like a compass needle
  by its wheel. Black Elk points North.
 Meek maintenance serves selfless ends.
We rise beyond our ego trips
with *Everysoul*, the beadle –
 barging in among her bevy of ships
  graceful as loons, that skim along the strands.

The serpent trails in silver toward its mouth.
  The river mingles death and birth
   within her sinuous
  continuum. Black Elk points South.
 Our sadness fades in memory of mirth –
that Delta *chelys*-turtleshell
has tuned a River-Horse
 to Ocean hymn : *all shall be well*

160

when AGAPE pilots each public oath.

The stars eddy their congregated lights
   in clouds, like candles lit for sup.
    They are high, and clear;
   we're here below. Black Elk points up.
Unfazed, our intellect takes flights...
All things are One. The human Image
is a bright mirror.
 Our happiness is, as that sage
  whispers, a *shalom*-shell of equal rights.

The Mississippi is a green bowl in the Earth
  assembling from wellsprings sweet
   all waters to their source
  again. Black Elk points to his feet.
 Rich is her round and rose-tinged girth,
 throned in fiery adamant;
strong is her life-force,
 wiser than any cruel intent
  of raging bullies to retard her birth.

*

Compared to proud urban giraffes, your turtle is not so
tall –
    four feet planted firmly on the ground,
     she marches over the sand
    to her nesting-mound.
   She is imperturbable, below the squall
  overhead – where the human tale
plays out (on land,
 on sea) between good and evil –
  one lunatic dream-battle (moonrise, fall).

   Midway across these states, a salience
    bumps up from Earth. A dome
     of clay. Cahokia –
    the door into a cthonic realm
   whose *verde* radiates from soil, from silence.
  Just over the river, an airy arc
accents Louisiana
  with a steel rainbow... to mark
   this turtleshell of sky and planet (sweet circumference).

   That wrestle, clenched within each human soul
    prefigures and outlasts each frame.
     A lonesome train crossroad;
    a trestle bridge above the stream.
   And so one simple painted oval croons for all.
  Fierce eagles spy the turtledove
chant her encircled code –
  whose octave, through a green alcove
   lifts dickering men from greed to commonweal.

*

My wordy enthusiasms drift like flotsam
   twirling past the riverbank.
      Benjamin Latrobe
   with bundle of sketches, walking the plank
   betwixt the Capitol dome, his feverish wisdom
 floats in stone canoe (past the Arch
to come). O Mind! To probe
 the master plan – to trace the *arc*
   in *architect*... the almond of Jerusalem!

Such vision guides all masons, carpenters –
   all builders of the common good.
      A beautiful conception
   crowns each milky neighborhood
   with intricate invention. Cantilevers
 justly tuned as tree-limbs
lift in unison
 to launch their breezy, rangy skims –
   Minnehaha variations... (leafy tiers).

The aim was Liberty. But not for princes
   in their own regard. You must unself
      yourself to find yourself,
   in love and charity. The Gulf
   beckons, with azure waves... her sunny glances
 semaphore, from Ocean River –
Milky Way, gold Alph.
 Realm of calm, cosmic splendor...
   fantailed canopy, or *Fonte Gaia*. Ark of Peace.

*

163

THE GREEN RADIUS

The last air of the year grows clear and cold.
  This flat sameness of midwestern earth
    gives an abstract logic,
    geometrical. The plainest math
  is simple, elegant. Ponder this fold :
 the ground of government is law.
The ground of law – thick
 clouds obscure it – is a sacred awe.
   Its thread binds heart and mind... to heaven's hold.

  We cannot live this premise as we should.
   A bull careens through every heart;
    an Old Man River
    veers – relentless serpent-dart –
  shattering showboats and cottonwood.
 One stave stands plumb against the flow –
one *douve*, forever
 twined by water-lily, so :
   Love's steadfast will toward the good.

  Gray skies blanket the mournful prairie.
   Buffalo seek warmth in flocks.
    Young children sigh;
    old peasants tally their hard knocks;
   poor unhoused refugees carry
  the toughest load. Callous, unjust,
the world's blind eye
 sleepwalks, tranced by a frozen crust
                    *

jusqu'une colombe flamboyante fait fondre toute la glace.

                    *

164

The cigarette that swallowed Notre Dame in flame
  revivified her in the end,
    as lightning over tamaracks
  renews the moss. Phoenix will bend
 her wings – and supernatural nature claim
 your dreams. She is an agate-stone,
is *Everysoul*, whose acts
 are god-like in creation...
  unknown soldier (no one knows her name).

  Galla Placidia's peaceful galaxy...
    the Face that beams down from the apse
      at Sant'Apollinare...
    emblems of a radius, that caps
  LOGOS and NUMEROS in one bright ecstasy.
  Sphere that Nicolas Cusanus rolled
(out of one starry
 thought) into the center of the world :
    Concord proceeds from *Union*, in *Equality*.

  Her charism is eucharistic, thus.
   A family Thanksgiving feast,
     in memory of one
    who played the Phoenix for the least
  of men, of women... (that means US).
  Now : behold that bright green ray
slanting from the sun
 over clay chanting heads. Array
   your *chelys* now, Persephone – here comes Jésus.

*

THE GREEN RADIUS

In my mind I stand among low pine hills
   in the north country, looking south.
      A silver serpent
      shines in sunlight, bearing both
   wrath and hope. Earth-heart, that spills
   tears, water, blood. *O what*
a dusty element
   is Man! cries out Hamlet –
      Guide us, Sant'Agata! *Pilot our wills.*

Close by, soft *Jonah*-woman sings.
   Her turtledove refrain is joined
      by swimming turtle clans
      curving small rainbow arcs – coined
   with pennies (Lincoln-*logos*... honeyed stings).
Here blood turns wine, and water, milk –
hot raging vengeance
   to forgiveness, mercy. Wise Black Elk
      rides through a snowdrift universe. *Love moves all things.*

The Word spins in its vortex. I would speak to you.
   Your unknown soldier will endure.
      The evil that men do
      cannot defile. His heart is pure.
   Your green *Rey*, like a wheat-grain, out of Ireland grew –
with malice toward none, with charity
for all – red white and blue.
   And in the distance, at the Gulf, I see
      that Friedheim turtle float home, free... (her shield
marked ÉCU).

12.3–12.12.23

166

Made in the USA
Monee, IL
09 January 2025

76480606R00111